MW00917392

THE DOOR IS OPEN

THE DOOR IS OPEN

STORIES OF CELEBRATION AND COMMUNITY BY 11 DESI VOICES

LITTLE, BROWN AND COMPANY
New York Boston

This book is a work of fiction. Names, characters, places, and incidents are the product of the author's imagination or are used fictitiously. Any resemblance to actual events, locales, or persons, living or dead, is coincidental.

Interior design by Carla Weise

Little, Brown and Company
Hachette Book Group
1290 Avenue of the Americas, New York, NY 10104
Visit us at LBYR.com

First Edition: April 2024

Little, Brown and Company is a division of Hachette Book Group, Inc. The Little, Brown name and logo are trademarks of Hachette Book Group, Inc.

The publisher is not responsible for websites (or their content) that are not owned by the publisher.

Little, Brown and Company books may be purchased in bulk for business, educational, or promotional use. For information, please contact your local bookseller or the Hachette Book Group Special Markets Department at special.markets@hbgusa.com.

Library of Congress Cataloging-in-Publication Data
Names: Khan, Hena, editor.
Title: The door is open / edited by Hena Khan.
Description: First edition. | New York : Little, Brown and Company, 2024. | Audience: Ages 8–12. | Summary: "A story of community, belonging, and friendship told by South Asian authors through an interconnected anthology, based in the fictional town of Maple Grove, New Jersey, and centralized at the town community center." —Provided by publisher.
Identifiers: LCCN 2023007020 | ISBN 9780316450638 (hardcover) | ISBN 9780316450836 (ebook)
Subjects: CYAC: South Asian Americans—Fiction. | Communities—Fiction. | New Jersey—Fiction. | Short stories. | LCGFT: Short stories.
Classification: LCC PZ5 .T555 2024 | DDC [Fic]—dc23
LC record available at https://lccn.loc.gov/2023007020

ISBNs: 978-0-316-45063-8 (hardcover)
978-0-316-45083-6 (ebook)

Printed in the United States of America

LSC-C

Printing 1, 2024

To everyone looking to find their place in the world

CONTENTS

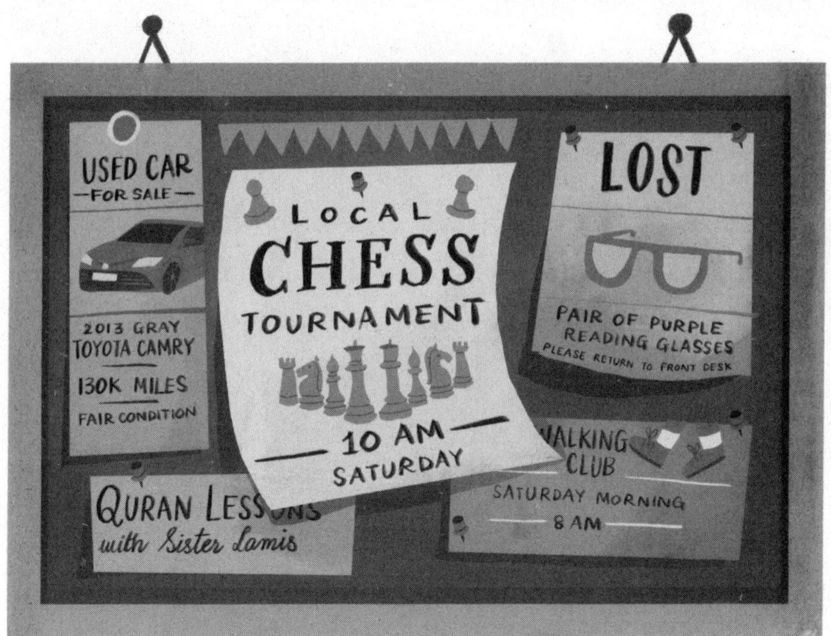

CHECK YOURSELF

by Veera Hiranandani

I PICK UP THE QUEEN AND TWIRL HER BETWEEN MY forefinger and thumb. I can see my path. My opponent has left his rook unguarded, and my queen can take it. It will leave my bishop open to his knight, but my other rook will take it if he does, so I'm protected. I make my move and look him in the eyes.

I once read that the queen wasn't always the most powerful piece on the chessboard. In fact, the queen didn't use to be the queen at all. She was only an advisor to the king, with very little power. Her power grew over the years, especially during the rise of Queen Isabella I in Spain, when chess traveled all the way from India, to Persia, and then to Europe. Queen Isabella sounded like a terrible person, though, because she forced all the Jews and Muslims to leave Spain. During that time, the queen chess piece started to change into what she is now. My queen is not like Isabella. My queen protects all her people.

The air sits still around us, and I can hear the creaking as my opponent leans forward in his wooden chair, studying the chessboard. He squints a little and rests his chin on his clasped hands as the steam of his coffee rises from the mug on the table. A few minutes go by.

"Well, Grandpa?" I say.

"It's a good move," he says, but then he moves his other knight and takes one of my pawns. "Check."

"Darn it," I say, and check. How did I not see his other knight just two moves away from my king? I scan my eyes over every spot on the board, drawing imaginary lines where each piece could go and to see what pieces they could capture. I try to stay a move or two ahead, but it's hard to think into the future like that. That's what the game of chess is about, though. The present, yes, but mostly it's about imagining the future.

The pieces are made from marble. My queen is black with little white marble veins running through her—all my pieces look like that. The pieces on Grandpa's side are white with little black veins running through them. He gave me the set last spring on my twelfth birthday. It's smooth and shiny, and the pieces have a nice heavy feel in my hand. Though sometimes I prefer the simple wooden board I bought with my own allowance when I first started to play. But I wouldn't tell Grandpa that.

I look at my queen again and now see that Grandpa's queen from all the way on the other side of the board can move in a straight diagonal and capture my king. How did I not notice? I squeeze my eyes shut and open them again. *Come on, Chaya*, I tell myself. *You're a better player than this.*

"Grandpa, I think I need a break," I say with a smile so he doesn't suspect the sinking feeling that is taking over my stomach.

"Okay," he says, "but we'll practice again tomorrow. You only have two days before the tournament." Then he leans back in his chair and repeats what he's said many times before. "Remember, don't think about the player. Think about what's happening on the board."

"I know, I know," I say lightly, but inside I still feel a weight in the bottom of my stomach. I pad in my sock feet toward Grandpa's cozy kitchen with its yellow table and white cabinets. He moved into the apartment down the street from our house ten years ago when my grandma died. I don't really remember her. Over the years, Grandpa taught me how to play chess, and now I stay at his apartment after school most days until Mom and Dad get home from work.

I rummage through the kitchen cabinets looking for the exact snack that will distract me from worrying about Saturday's tournament. It's the final local tournament, and whoever wins will compete for the state chess championship. Last year, I lost to Andrew Pierson in the final game and I haven't stopped thinking about it since. Though I do think about the board, I also think about the player—well, particularly one player: Andrew.

I probably wouldn't win state anyway, because New Jersey's pretty competitive. I just want to beat him. I can't stand the way he struts around at chess club giving everyone tips they didn't even ask for. It's like he thinks he invented the game.

I find the snack I am looking for in the back on the bottom shelf—soup nuts. Grandpa usually saves them for soup, but I like to eat them straight out of the can. Soup nuts are not even nuts at all, but puffy little round crackers that are kind of crunchy and a little bit salty. They remind me of cold winter days and Jewish holidays when my mom makes matzo ball soup. My dad likes them too, even though he was born in India and didn't grow up eating them like my mom did. I open the can and stuff a big handful in my mouth.

"Blah!" I say with my mouth full. I run over to the garbage and spit them out. "Gross!"

"What?" Grandpa says as he comes into the kitchen.

"These are so stale," I say as I wipe my mouth. I grab a glass, fill it with water, and take a big gulp, washing away the stale taste. Then I look at the expiration date.

"Grandpa, these expired a year ago!"

He waves his hand. "I don't pay attention to those dates. They just want you to throw out perfectly good food and buy more."

"I don't think that's true, Grandpa. I feel like I've just been poisoned," I say, and put my hand around my neck, sticking out my tongue.

"Oh, you're fine," he says. "Stale soup nuts never poisoned anyone."

He finds a box of chocolate chip cookies, peers through his thick glasses, and reads the side of the package. “These don’t expire until a month from now, so eat up.”

I smile and we both dig into the cookies.

Later that night, at dinner, as I push around the aloo gobi and rice on my plate, I can’t stop thinking about the game Grandpa and I never finished and that I would have probably lost.

“What’s wrong?” my mother asks.

I shrug and take a bite of rice.

“School okay?” she asks.

I nod.

“How was Grandpa’s?”

“Fine,” I say.

“Nervous about the tournament?” she says.

“Nah,” I say.

My dad looks up from his food. “I’ll play a game with you tonight,” he says, and wipes his mouth.

“That’s okay, Dad. I’m good. Thanks, though.”

He nods, and then he and my mom start

talking about their workdays, which can get boring, so I head upstairs, grabbing more cookies on the way. If I tell them I'm nervous, they'll go into very annoying problem-solving action, and the truth is my dad's not the greatest chess player. I always beat him. My mom's a little better, because Grandpa taught her, but she never seems to have time to play.

That night, my belly full of too many cookies, I lie on my bed and imagine the future. I imagine beating Andrew. I think about the last game of the tournament, everyone else tired and disappointed and Andrew and I facing off. I think about the moment when I can say "Checkmate," and his cheeks turn a little red. I think about standing up, being a good sport, shaking his hand, and how he would have to shake my hand, smile, and be gracious. Then I think of calmly walking to the bathroom, making sure I'm alone, and punching my fist in the air with a burst of glory so delicious, I'll coast on it for months.

I feel a little mean, thinking all of this, but I

heard Andrew say once that a girl had never beat him, which first of all isn't true because I've beat him in chess club practice games and so has Maha Iqbal. So, if he's going to lie like that, maybe he deserves to lose to one of us, the only two girls in chess club. Because there aren't as many girls, some people (mostly boys) think that girls aren't as good at chess. I know that's not true, but the only way to prove it is for one of us to win the tournament.

Thinking about this, I try extra hard with Grandpa the next day after school and manage to beat him in three out of the five games we play.

"You're ready, Chaya, and no matter what happens, you're doing it because you love the game."

"I don't know. Yesterday was a mess."

"Just nerves. If you stay focused like today, you'll be golden."

"Thanks, Grandpa," I say, and we fist-bump. I hope he's right.

Saturday morning comes, the day of the tournament. Mom makes my power breakfast: scrambled eggs and buttered wheat toast because she says the protein in the eggs and the fat in the butter will keep my energy steady. I force myself to eat it even though my nerves rattle through my body.

She drops me off at the Maple Grove Community Center, which I've played at many times. I love having tournaments here because I know exactly how they're set up and the main room has nice high ceilings and big windows. Sometimes I've had to play in much smaller rooms or hot and musty school basement spaces, which make me feel like I can't breathe, especially if things aren't going well.

"Good luck! We're here for you no matter what happens," my mom says, but I can see the hope in her eyes. She's hoping I win, not just for me, but because she knows how grumpy I get for days when I lose a big tournament.

"Thanks, Mom," I say, and shiver a little at the cold air that hits my face. I walk in and see a big sign in black marker—THE FUTURE OF THE COMMUNITY CENTER IS IN OUR HANDS! TOWN HALL MEETING

NEXT THURSDAY!—which makes me more nervous. I'm not sure what's going on with the center, but I push these thoughts out of my head. *Focus, Chaya.*

I wish Grandpa were here, but they don't let parents or grandparents or any guests of the players watch, which is probably for the best. The times my mom watches practice games, she makes all these concerned faces if I'm losing and happy faces if I'm winning. My dad tries to focus but glazes over at a certain point, so I'm either worried that they're paying too much attention or too little. But when Grandpa watches me play, he's in the story of every game just like I am, wondering how it's going to end.

Every chess game has its own story. Some games start out bold and fast, some slow and careful. The pieces have different personalities, depending on who's playing them. There are little pawns who become fierce and overwhelming, chipping away the opposing forces like death from a thousand papercuts. There are subtle, sneaky queens and assertive ones and hyper ones. There are quiet, cowardly kings hiding behind everyone else, and kings who do their best to support everyone working hard to protect them. Then of course there are the rest of the supporting pieces, who are all important.

Though I love the queen, because who doesn't, my favorite piece is the knight. The knight has the most unexpected move. It can fly. Well, not actually fly, but jump over other pieces to reach its destination. The knight, especially for newer players, is often the piece you don't see coming.

I put my backpack in a locker, check in, and look at the pairing list. Then I find the table for my first game. I sit down, glad my opponent isn't there yet, and take in the room. The familiar smell is comforting to me, a combination of polished wood floors, coffee, and the orange-scented soap used in the bathrooms. My first opponent is Ben Geller.

"Hi," he says. I say a quick hi back, but I don't smile. I like to keep it serious while I play. I beat Ben pretty quickly and play a few more easy games. In the beginning, the lowest-ranked players are matched against the highest-ranked players, and usually by the end of the tournament, only the strongest players are left playing each other.

During the lunch break, I go and find my secret spot on the basement floor down a long hallway. It's dark and quiet. I don't like to talk to people during a tournament. It makes me feel too competitive, and I start getting distracted by thoughts of winning rather than paying attention to the story on the board, as Grandpa says. Even so, I've kept my eye on Andrew and Maha, and they also beat out the lower-ranked players.

I sit and eat my energy bar and apple and imagine different chess openings. I try not to think about Andrew, but it's impossible. When I finish, I get up and hear some kids talking. I freeze at the sound of their voices and stand back behind the corner of the hallway. Then I peek around, hoping they can't see me. It's Andrew, Ben, and another kid, Aiden. What are they doing down here?

"Maha and Chaya are the ones to beat. I've lost to them both today," says Ben.

"Well, I'm about to go up against them after lunch, so their winning streak will end," says Andrew.

"Be careful. You've got to watch out for those Indian girls," Aiden says. "They're good at that kind of stuff."

"What do you mean?" Ben says.

"You know, math, chess, science, computers. They're all good at that stuff."

"Maybe," Andrew says. "But I can beat any girl who comes my way, Indian or not."

"Not if I beat them first," Aiden says.

Ben just shrugs, but my heart is pounding so hard, I feel the thudding in my ears.

"Do you have the magic?" Aiden asks.

"Yup," Ben says, and takes three cans of Mountain Dew out of his bag. What's so special about Mountain Dew?

"Bring on the sugar rush," Andrew says. "Those girls are going down for sure." Then they all clink the cans together and chug the soda.

I duck back behind the wall while they finish

and wait for them to go back upstairs. My head is spinning with everything I've just heard. First, they think Maha and I are good at chess only because of our Indian background, even though Maha's family is from Pakistan. Second, they think we're not as good at chess because we're girls. Third, they drink some stupid sugary soda because they think it will make them better at chess!

I take a few deep breaths to calm myself down, something my father taught me. I count for five on the inhale and five on the exhale. After I do it a few times, I feel more relaxed, more like myself. I think again of Aiden's words—the part about being Indian and good at chess. I didn't even know that was a thing people thought.

I usually like things that make me feel more Indian because only my father is Indian. Sometimes when I'm around people who have two Indian parents, I don't feel Indian enough, almost like I'm pretending. But I don't want anyone to think that I'm good at chess just because of my Indian background.

I look at the clock on the wall. I have to be back in the main room in five minutes. I lift my arms over my head and stretch, then pick up my backpack and head upstairs. It seems like Andrew and his friends don't want to give me, the actual *person* I am, credit for being good at chess. I'm either not good enough because I'm a girl or too good because I'm Indian. What would they think about the fact that my Jewish grandfather is the one who taught me how to play?

As I enter the main room, again the wooden, soapy smell comforts me. The pairing list says I'm up against Aiden. I walk over to the assigned table and sit down, and we face each other. I nod with laser eyes. He returns my nod.

"Prepare to go down," he says.

"Nice chess etiquette," I say sarcastically, but then regret it. The last thing I need is to get into an argument with Aiden. Luckily, he doesn't respond. We start, and I decide to play extra fast. Maybe it's because of the adrenaline running through my veins because of what happened downstairs, or the knot of anger that's growing inside me, but after I capture his rook, it doesn't take me long to see the move that will win the game—just me, Chaya, being good at something because I am. My bishop and a pawn have trapped his king after moving him into the corner with my queen.

"Checkmate," I say after only twenty minutes, and press my lips together so I won't smile. This game is a quick story, ending before it really began. Aiden abruptly stands up and shakes my hand, though he doesn't look me in the eyes. His hand feels a little clammy with a slight tremble to it. I want to tell him, "Maybe next time, don't drink so much Mountain Dew," but I don't. I have to focus on the next round, because Andrew just beat Maha.

Suddenly my own hands feel clammy and shaky. I look over at Maha, and she gives me a little secret thumbs-up. I smile and nod. Then we turn away quickly. It's nice she's encouraging me even though she lost. We're friends in chess club, but we don't talk during tournaments. It's a kind of silent understanding we have. Maybe it's because we don't want to act like we're part of a "girls' team." We just want to be seen as two separate kids, playing chess.

I wipe my hands on my jeans and again wish Grandpa were here to give me the look he has in his eyes when we play, the look that tells me no matter what happens, he's always rooting for me.

Andrew and I sit down at the same time. I usually try to look my opponent in the eyes right away, but this time when I look at him, I see one corner of his mouth turned up into a slight smile and it sends me back to an hour ago, listening to him in the hallway. So I keep my eyes down and think of Grandpa's words: *Don't try to beat the person. Just focus on the board.*

I'm playing white this time. Chess rules say the white pieces always go first, though I'm not sure who made up that rule. It means I have the advantage, because I won against a higher-ranked player than Andrew did, but now I feel even more pressure. When you play white, you're supposed to win.

I start out moving my pawn in the e4 space and decide to follow with my knights. Andrew will probably do the same, and our four knights will be in a sort of face-off. Grandpa says the real game happens in the center of the board, during the middle part. And I agree. It's what my chess teacher says at the club, too. But the pieces waiting in the corners and on the edges can be just as powerful, even if they're not in the center, even if they get forgotten sometimes. In certain games, they're the most powerful pieces of all.

But right now, Andrew is moving his pieces aggressively. He's got his queen on my side of the board. He's already taken several pawns and a bishop and I'm down several points. I turn my head from side to side, stretching my neck, and try to ignore what's coming—that dreaded last-game-of-the-tournament moment. It's the moment when my adrenaline starts to drop and my breathing slows and I remember that I've been playing chess all day. My limbs start to feel heavy and my eyes burn. I just want to go home, have dinner with my family, and feel safe.

This time I look up at Andrew to see if he's losing his energy, and what does he do? He winks at me. It feels like someone has just dropped a handful of ice down my back.

"Check," he says.

I frantically eye the board. I've lost sight of the future. He's got his rook aimed straight at my king. I need to move my king, but then I see my knight next to my king, waiting for me. I haven't touched it in a while and can use it to launch over Andrew's pawn and take his rook. That will open up my bishop, and then I can put him in check with my queen.

We play a few more moves, and I do put him in check. People who have finished their games start to watch us. Andrew clears his throat loudly. I see the sweat glisten on his forehead. He meets my eyes again, and I can tell how much he wants to beat me—not my pieces, but *me.* If he moves one way, I have a plan to win. If he moves another, he might win. The future is unknown.

I start to think about why this game matters so much. The reason it matters to Mom and Dad is because they know I want to win. It matters to Grandpa because he knows I'll learn something no matter what happens. I already beat Aiden, showing him that girls can beat him. If I lose to Andrew, will it show him that maybe people with Indian backgrounds aren't always good at things like chess? Maybe, but I don't want that to be the story of this game.

Instead, he makes the move I hoped he would. Now I have the future all planned out. After two moves, I say, "Checkmate."

Andrew's face falls and his cheeks turn red. I almost wonder if he's going to cry. But then he straightens his shoulders, takes a deep breath, and stands up slowly.

"Nice game," he says in a low voice, and holds out his hand. He even manages a small smile.

A part of me still wants to shake him by the

shoulders and say, "But what about all that ridiculous stuff you said downstairs about girls and Indian people while guzzling Mountain Dew?" Instead I decide to let the game speak for itself.

"Thank you," I say, and accept his handshake. Then I do one last thing: I wink at him. He blinks and moves his head back like he's startled and quickly turns toward the back of the room, where Aiden and Ben are waiting for him. His shoulders drop a bit as he walks away. Aiden and Ben give him a nudge in the arm and a pat on the back, but Andrew doesn't look at them. He just stares straight ahead and keeps walking.

When I leave the community center I see Grandpa, Mom, and Dad near the front steps waving to me. I keep my gold trophy behind my back and watch each one of them, their faces looking at me, searching for the end of the story. I know they all hope for the same ending, but for different reasons. I hold out my trophy toward them. The gold glints in the late-afternoon sun and their faces light up.

"Fantastic!" Dad says, and claps.

"You did it!" Mom says, and holds her arms out for a hug.

"You were ready," Grandpa says, and squeezes my shoulder.

They all surround me, and it feels even better than pumping my fist in the air alone in the bathroom. But this is just the ending of today's story. Tomorrow, in the future, all the parts of me that make me who I am will start a new one.

ALOK AT THE DANCE

by Maulik Pancholy

I TUG AT THE COLLAR OF MY POLO SHIRT AND JIGGLE my leg inside my khaki pants so hard that my knee bangs up against my desk.

I stare at the clock behind Mr. Markham's head.

Is the minute hand *stuck*?

"What are some factors that drive immigration

to the United States?" Mr. Markham drones from behind his desk. "Did anyone do the reading?"

I squeeze my eyes shut, but when I pop them back open, the minute hand still hasn't moved. I'm starting to sweat. Could there be a glitch in the clock's machinery? That might prevent the bell from ringing? What if it never goes off, and *I'm stuck here forever*?

"Alok? Any ideas?" Mr. Markham asks.

"Huh?" I almost shriek in surprise.

"Was that a squeal of excitement I heard?" Mr. Markham deadpans. "And over seventh-grade history, no less?"

Shoot. I was only half paying attention. "I'm sorry, can you repeat the question?"

"Immigration," Mr. Markham says with a sigh. "Why are people compelled—"

"Oh, right," I say. "Well—" But before I can finish, an earsplitting ring fills the classroom.

"It's Fridaaaaay!" someone yells.

I'm halfway up the aisle, racing toward the door, when Mr. Markham calls out, "If you didn't do the reading, be sure to look at it over the weekend! We're having a quiz on Monday!"

Mom's car is already waiting in the carpool line. My older sister, Shilpa, is hunched over the steering wheel, blowing a bubble with her hot pink chewing gum. It smacks against her lips.

"Ugh, Shilpa's driving? *Again?*" I throw my bookbag into the back seat.

"She's a good driver." Mom cranes around and tries to pinch my cheek. "Besides, she has to practice."

"She's so slow!" I whine. "Why does she have to drive *today*? I want to get home so we can change and get to the center on time!"

"Why are you always so annoying?" Shilpa shoots me a warning look in the rearview mirror. She presses the button to lower her window, glaring at me the whole time as it whirs its descent. Then she reaches her hand out the window and sticks a magnetic STUDENT DRIVER pop-up sign onto the roof of the car.

We lurch forward, nearly rear-ending the station wagon in front of us.

Shilpa's amateur driving skills—I mean, who brakes for a stop sign two blocks before you can even read the word "stop"?—threatens to add on, like, twenty minutes to our ride home.

I press my lips together, trying not to be what Dad calls a "back seat driver." Anyhow, I'm pretty sure if I said another word, Shilpa would drive even slower just to annoy me.

Last year—on this very day—Shilpa and I were in the back seat *together*, excitedly planning out our outfits for the night and practicing our dance moves.

Now, it's like the eleventh grade has snatched up my sister and sent back this strange clone of her.

I try to cope by planning my outfit for the night.

See, tonight's the beginning of the festival of Navratri. Which literally means "nine nights." Throughout India—for nine nights—people celebrate the various forms of the goddess Durga.

In Gujarat, where my family's from, Navratri is a *huge* deal.

Instead of Durga, some people call her Ambe Maa or Shakti based on different traditions. But whatever name you use, she is totally awesome. She rides a muscular lion and wields all these weapons over her head—rooting out evil and spreading good. She protects the entire universe.

Which is a pretty cool job, if you ask me.

And the best part of Navratri is that we celebrate by dancing. I'm not talking, like, two-stepping at the middle school semiformal. I mean dances where people bang dandiyas over their heads and where we clap and stomp our feet on the ground until we're dripping with sweat.

In Gujarat, people literally spill out into the streets, wearing their brightest colors, forming rings of thousands of people playing garba and staying up until all hours of the night.

And here in New Jersey, we fill the entire floor of the Maple Grove Community Center banquet hall.

I'm planning to dazzle on that floor tonight. In the outfit I've been planning in my head for an entire week now.

No thanks to Shilpa.

I guess she's got more important things to do than hang with me now.

"Watch where you're going!" Mom shrieks.

Shilpa almost drives straight into our mailbox.

The three of us head into Mom and Dad's room. I sit cross-legged on the bed while Mom throws open the double doors to her armoire. The sweet smell of sandalwood and mothballs fills the air. Behind me, Shilpa scrolls through text messages on her phone, still smacking her gum.

Mom's armoire is where she stores all her Indian stuff, like saris neatly folded into stacks and jewelry tucked inside velvet boxes. And on the top shelf are old family albums, filled with black-and-white pictures of my grandparents from when they first moved to America.

Sometimes, when my grandparents come over

for dinner, Mom will bring out the albums. And long after we've finished eating, my grandparents will still be telling Shilpa and me stories about what it was like in New Jersey back then. There weren't as many other Indian families living here yet, so sometimes my nana and nani would get homesick for all the relatives and friends they had left behind in India.

But, over time, they built their own community.

Our community. In Maple Grove.

"Your nana and nani came here to study, to expand their opportunities," Mom likes to say, her hand resting on Nani's shoulder.

"Which is why you kids need to study hard, too!" Dad always echoes, trying to ruffle Shilpa's hair.

A dinging noise pulls me back to reality. It's a text message on Shilpa's phone.

"Who's that?" I ask.

"None of your business!" She bugs out her eyes at me, literally scooting two feet over on the bed.

"How can you even be on your phone right

now?" I throw both my hands up in the air. "Mom's about to bring out our clothes for the night!"

"Why do you care about *clothes* so much, anyway?" she says. And the way she says it makes me feel like...

I don't know. Like maybe she means something else.

The two feet between us on the bed seems to grow even wider.

"Can we have one afternoon of no bickering, *please*?" Mom asks.

She pulls out a colorful stack of chaniya cholis from the armoire and unfurls two of them for Shilpa. One is bright yellow, and the other's a deep red. They're both covered in patterns stitched in shiny silver and gold thread.

"Which one do you want to wear, Shilpa?" Mom asks.

Shilpa's eyes perk up ever so slightly as she runs a finger along the hem of each dress. And for a second, it seems like she's going to ask me for my opinion. But then, she glances at her phone and mumbles, "Minu and Tinu said red's totally in this year. So, red." She tugs on her gum. A long pink strand dips between her fingers and her mouth.

I consider making a smart remark about being a follower, but Mom's already pulling out more clothes. This time for me.

"How about you, Alok? What do you want to wear?"

Of course, I know exactly what I'm going to say. "My teal blue kurta, please, with the gold vest. And the dhoti pants with the gold embroidery around the ankles. You know. The ones that sparkle!"

Dad waltzes in, unbuttoning his blue Oxford dress shirt and wriggling his arm out of the sleeve.

"Are you planning to change, too, Arvind?" Mom asks.

"Of course I'm changing!" Dad pumps his fists in the air, wriggling his shoulders like he's already on the dance floor. "I always get dressed up for Navratri!" He heads into their walk-in closet.

But when he comes back, he's buttoning up

what looks like the exact same blue dress shirt. Except this one has faint, thin white pinstripes.

I stare down at the shiny teal material in my hands. "That's what you're wearing?" I ask hesitantly. I glance at Shilpa, but her head's still buried in her phone.

"Well, I don't want to steal your thunder!" Dad laughs. Then he wriggles his shoulders all over again. "You better go get changed so we can start dancing!"

Mom smiles. "Yeah, Alok! I thought you wanted to get to the center early!"

I grab my kurta and race up the stairs.

The parking lot is already packed when we pull in. As I open my car door, I can hear the thumping music that spills out of the center: the steady beat of a drum and a chorus of high-pitched voices rings out over the melody of a harmonium. The rhythm's slow. For now.

But it'll be racing by the end of the night.

I chew my nails in anticipation, just thinking about how fast it'll get.

Shilpa's infamous friends, Minu and Tinu, saunter our way, the bells on their ankles tinkling as they head across the parking lot. Minu and Tinu are twins, and if you ask me, they give the evil stepsisters in *Cinderella* a run for their money.

I tug on Shilpa's chaniya, watching Mom and Dad head into the hall. "Let's go!" I say. "The dancing's already started!"

"Stop pulling on me!" Shilpa grabs her chaniya out of my hand.

Minu chortles, and I feel my face grow hot. Tinu scowls at me, but then she points to a row of cars parked near the basketball nets. "Hey, Shilpa. Look. Who's. Here." She takes an emphatic pause between each word.

I follow their gaze to see Dinesh.

Dinesh is sixteen and a junior at the high school. At the moment, he's leaned up against the dented front bumper of a beat-up gray Toyota Camry. He wears a plain white kurta with white churidar pants that are so tight, I can see his calf muscles nearly popping out of them. I try not to stare at his legs as he tosses a set of car keys up and down in one hand.

Tinu lets out a dreamy sigh. "His dad just bought him that car," she says. "From a used car lot. Isn't it *so* sweet how much he loves it?"

Minu nods, her breathlessness matching Tinu's. "Everything about him is the coolest."

Shilpa clears her throat and leans in. Her voice comes out all weird. "If my parents ever get me a car of my own, I want one just like that."

I cock my head at her. "Really? *That's* the car you want? An old Toyota Camry with a bunch of dents in it?"

I see the red rising up her cheeks. "I thought you were going inside!" she screeches. "Why are you even still here?"

Now Minu and Tinu slowly start circling me, like a pair of snakes.

Tinu pats my head. She singsongs, "I think *I* know why he's still here."

"Why?" I ask, ducking out from under her hand.

Minu pokes me in the ribs. "Does someone else here think Dinesh is cute, too?"

"What?" I try to dodge her probing fingers. I look up to Shilpa for help, but she presses her lips into a thin, tight line.

Tinu pats my head again. "Yeah, Alok. Is there something you want to tell us?" She pinches the collar of my gold vest. "Did you dress to impress Dinesh tonight?"

My face falls. "No! I mean . . . what are you even talking about?" I turn on my heels and race toward the community center. I think I hear Minu or Tinu, or maybe even Shilpa—who can tell, because they all sound exactly the same now—laugh. "Poor little guy! He'll figure it out someday!"

I head inside, and the pounding of the dhol drowns out their voices.

The center is already hopping to the steady beat of a tran tali. In Gujarati, "tran" means "three" and "tali" means "clap," and a tran tali is, well, a dance with three claps. The three beats stay constant, so what's fun is that you can improvise around it.

The parents are dancing in a large ring that takes up the entire perimeter of the floor. They dance slow and steady, clapping right on the beat. Which is so like the parents. They're not really into changing things up.

I push past their circle and almost run smack-dab into my mom and Nani dancing next to each other. I wave, and Nani blows me a kiss.

A group of girls Shilpa's age have formed their own circle just inside the parents' ring. They twirl themselves around on every third clap, making their chaniyas billow around their legs.

Even closer to the center, a bunch of kids my age have formed yet another group. Instead of twirling, they're hiking up their knees and clapping overhead. I spot my friend Rohit and jump in behind him.

"You wore a dhoti, dude? Nice!" he says. He pauses mid-dance to admire my outfit, even though he's dressed just like Dad. He has on gray dress pants and a light blue button-down that he's already starting to sweat through. He pushes up his gold-rimmed glasses onto his nose. "Wanna play some basketball later?" he asks, resuming his moves.

I shrug. "Maybe. But let's dance first."

And that's when I see her. Or, rather, a painting of her.

At the very center of the dance floor is a round table covered in a gold tablecloth. A large picture frame rests on top, surrounded by votive candles.

It's the goddess Durga.

Her face is calm, but she looks fierce in her bright red sari. The lion at her feet is mid-roar, and her ten arms reach wide around her, each of her hands clasped tightly around a different weapon. Her sword is at the very top, arching over her head.

The dhol bangs a downbeat, and the pace of the music picks up. I have one knee in the air, and my hands are over my head, when Rohit says,

"Let's get out of here and play some b-ball with the guys, yeah?"

"Now?" I wipe the sweat off my brow. "It's just getting good!"

"This'll go on for hours." He pulls me out of the circle. "Come on!"

I exhale through my nose and follow him out.

Rohit drags me toward a mini basketball court sandwiched between a bunch of parked cars. A group of kids are already mid-game.

"Let's join," Rohit says.

Dinesh's car is parked right on the edge of the court, and a handful of guys are swarmed around him, hanging on his every word. The hood is open, and as we pass by them I hear Dinesh say, "Yeah! I'm gonna take this engine apart and rebuild the whole thing. Soup this baby up, you know?" The guys all nod, entranced.

Rohit steps into the game, and I follow behind him. I like basketball. I'm good at it, too. But we can shoot hoops any old day at school. Navratri is only nine nights of the year, and in Maple Grove, we don't even get to celebrate it for nine nights. We only rent the community center for two weekends: that's two Fridays and two Saturdays. I mean, a lot of other stuff happens at the center: spelling bees, weddings, even chess matches. But for Navratri, this is all we get.

I look longingly back at the hall.

"Alok!" Rohit calls, and passes me the basketball.

I catch it and start dribbling.

Now I get why Rohit is dressed like Dad. It isn't easy to play basketball in a kurta that hangs to my knees and a dhoti swathed around my legs like two giant laundry bags. I hike the material up with one hand and dribble closer to the basket with the other. One of the other kids, Ajay, swipes at the ball, trying to knock it out of my hands.

Rohit raises his arm. "Over here!"

But Ajay's relentless. Every time I try to pass the ball, Ajay's right there, his hands ready to steal.

I dribble forward, and Ajay pops in front of

me. I try to dribble back, and his elbow edges up along my ribs. He's like an octopus.

"Gonna give her a sweet new carburetor, too," I hear Dinesh brag, just as I finally manage to fake Ajay out.

At last, I have a clear shot at Rohit. I heave the ball with all my might. But the gold-embroidered ankle of my dhoti snags on my chappals. My body twists.

The ball goes flying out of my hands and barrels in the opposite direction.

Fast.

Straight toward Dinesh's car.

I see a wave of confusion pass over Dinesh's eyes as his jaw drops. Anuj, on his right, claps his hand over his mouth, and Niam, on his left, falls to his knees and screams, "Iiiincoooomiiiiing!"

There's a whooshing sound from the ball, and then a metallic thud as it crashes into the front bumper on the passenger side. The hood of the Camry crashes closed.

Then it bounces back open.

Then it slams closed one last time.

The basketball rolls to a stop at Dinesh's feet.

For a moment, everything is dead silent.

Then Dinesh tilts his head toward the sky. He yells, and it seems to echo off the side of the community center. "Did you *aim* that at my brand-new car?"

"No!" I squeal. I'm shaking so hard, I'm afraid I might pee my pants. "I promise! I got tangled in my dhoti! It was an accident!"

Dinesh starts heading toward me, a group of kids right behind him.

"You dented my bumper!" he screams, and it sounds like there are flames somewhere deep inside his belly trying to erupt out of his mouth. "What's the matter with you?"

"It was already dented!" As soon as I say it, I'm one hundred percent sure it was the wrong thing to say. But now I can't seem to stop myself. "I mean, there are dents all over that car!"

"What did you say?" he roars. "Don't you dare talk about Mildred that way!"

A gasp goes up from all the kids.

“Who’s...? Wait, what?” I stammer. “Who’s Mildred?”

Dinesh grabs the front of my kurta in his fist and lifts me off the ground. One of my chappals slides off my foot.

“Mildred’s the name of my car!” Dinesh’s teeth are clenched tightly together.

His face is an inch away from mine now, and I can feel the heat coming off his breath. A single bead of sweat drips down his brow.

“Really?” I ask, in a voice so small it surprises even me. “You named your car...*Mildred*?”

A few kids snicker behind me.

“Yeah! I did!” Dinesh seems even angrier than before. He grips my kurta tighter. “You got a problem with that?”

Then, from somewhere off to my left, I hear Shilpa’s voice calling out. “Get your hands off my brother!”

I turn to see her running toward us, her red chaniya flying up around her ankles.

A look of surprise crosses Dinesh's face, and he unfurls his fist, setting me back down on the ground.

"What do you think you're doing?" Shilpa gets up in his face. "He's half your size! You think it's okay to pick on kids who are smaller than you?"

Behind Shilpa, I see Minu and Tinu looking on, their jaws dropped.

Dinesh raises his palms up in front of his chest. "Hold on! He dented my car!"

"He *dented* your car?" Shilpa asks, as if Dinesh just said the most absurd thing she's ever heard. She looks over her shoulder at his Camry. "Your car looks exactly the same as it did when you drove it in here!" Then she adds, "Tell me I'm wrong!"

Dinesh takes a step backward. He looks at, well, Mildred. We all do. He grunts. I see the muscle in his jaw ripple. Then, he spins back around and shoots me a menacing look. "Yeah? Maybe it does! But you better be more careful next time! And learn how to play basketball!"

I nod quickly, feeling everyone's eyes still

on me. I'm tempted to defend my basketball skills, but Shilpa's already grabbing my arm. She pulls me across the parking lot, away from the crowd.

I hear the tinkling of ankle bracelets as Minu and Tinu come running up behind us.

"Why on earth would you talk to Dinesh like that, Shilpa?" Minu asks. "It sounds like Alok's the one who started it!"

"Yeah, what were you thinking?" Tinu says. "Not cool. Not cool at all!"

"Can you give us a minute, please?" Shilpa keeps walking, and I do my best to keep up with her.

We find an empty parking spot and both sit on the curb stop. The music from the center still echoes into the parking lot, but it's like I barely hear it. I guess I'm still in shock from having just been manhandled by Dinesh.

We sit quietly for a minute, both of us catching our breaths.

Then Shilpa asks, "You all right?"

"Mm-hmm." I nod.

There's a little more silence. I look up at her and mumble begrudgingly, "Thanks."

She doesn't respond. And then I find myself muttering, "Although, honestly, I'm kinda surprised you helped me at all."

She pulls her gum out of her mouth and sticks it under the curb stop. "What's that supposed to mean? Of course I helped you. You're my brother."

"I know, but..." I swallow. "I mean...you've made it pretty clear that you just want me to leave you alone tonight."

"Well, that doesn't mean I'm not going to help you."

I hang my head. I take a breath. And then I say, "But, like...*why* do you want me to leave you alone?" Before she can answer, I add, "I mean, we used to get so excited about Navratri. About picking out our clothes. And dancing! But it seems like you're annoyed with me all the time now. Including today!"

Shilpa scoffs. “Excuse me?” She shakes her head. “It’s not like you’re so nice to me, either!”

“What’s that supposed to mean?”

“Oh really, Alok?” Her eyebrows fly up in surprise. “This was you today!” She makes a whiny voice, imitating me. “ ‘Shilpa’s so slow! Why does she have to drive?’ ”

And now it’s Shilpa’s turn to mutter. “Getting behind the wheel of *three thousand* pounds of metal is scary, okay? Just wait until it’s your turn!”

My eyes widen. I guess I never considered that Shilpa might be *scared.* I just thought...well, I guess I just thought that she was a bad driver.

“I’m sorry,” I finally say, quietly. And I have a feeling I should just leave it at that, but instead what bubbles out of me is “But at least I don’t make fun of you in front of your friends!”

A questioning look crosses Shilpa’s face. Then she lowers her gaze. “Do you mean what happened with Minu and Tinu earlier?” She swallows, and before I can answer she says, “I’m sorry about that, Alok. I promise, I wasn’t laughing at you when they were. I mean it. But..." She bites her lip. "I'm sorry I didn't stick up for you, either. Ugh. They were being so...*aggressive* tonight. And..." She takes a breath. "Well...I want you to know that if, like...if you *do* think Dinesh is cute. Or, not just Dinesh, but like, *guys*...it's totally fine. Okay?" Then, more quickly, she says, "I just mean, if you ever want to talk about anything like that. With me. You can. And...I'm sorry if I haven't made you feel that way before."

I feel something dip way down inside my belly.

My lips part, but nothing comes out.

I'm not sure I'm ready to talk about stuff like that with anyone yet.

Luckily, the sound of footsteps interrupts us.

It's Dinesh. His white kurta glows in the moonlight.

There's a sheepish expression on his face, and as he walks up to us, he says, "Yo. I'm really sorry about all that back there. I didn't mean to get so upset. I just...Mildred's my baby, you know?" He catches himself. "Which, I know, still doesn't make it right. I really shouldn't have done that. Are you okay, Alok?"

I nod. "I'm okay. And I'm sorry, too. Is the bumper really bad? Do I need to—?"

"We're cool," Dinesh says. "I need to replace that whole thing anyway."

Shilpa arches an eyebrow. "Wait. Did you just say *Mildred*?"

"Sure did." There's a grin on Dinesh's face. "Pretty cool name, right? It means 'strength.' I had a whole list of names picked out when we went to the used car lot. Pushpa, Mili, Jean, Rita. But when I saw Mildred, I was like, *Yo.* You're *a Mildred.*"

"Huh." Shilpa ponders. "I like it."

Dinesh's grin spreads even wider. "Really? Cool. Hey, listen. Can I make this up to the two of you?" He snaps his fingers. "Like, wait! Maybe I could take you both for a ride in Mildred sometime?"

Shilpa's eyes turn into saucers, and I'm pretty sure she's picturing the look on Minu's and Tinu's faces when she tells them what Dinesh just offered.

"Think about it." He shrugs. "Anyway. Are

you two planning on dancing? I'm pretty sure they've started the dandiya raas!"

My ears tune in to the music, and I know instantly that Dinesh is right. This is my favorite part of the night. The music is so much faster than it was when we first got here, and on every beat, there's the thump of dandiyas banging up against dandiyas.

I try to play it cool, but it's hard to hide the excitement in my voice. "I'd be down to dance."

"Well then." Dinesh cocks his head. "Should we all dance together?"

As the three of us head into the center, Shilpa nudges my arm and I nudge hers back. Then I whisper, "I didn't wear this to impress Dinesh. I wore it 'cause it's gonna look so good on the dance floor."

Shilpa grins. "You look amazing."

We grab dandiyas from the plastic tubs on the folding table just inside the door. To dance dandiya raas, you need a partner, someone to hit sticks with. You trade partners as the dance goes on, but you have to start as a pair.

I scan the room, trying to find a fourth for

our group. My grandmother is sitting in a row of folding chairs, talking with her friends. I run over. "Nani? Will you come dance with us?"

"Me? No, no! Take someone younger! You can dance harder that way!" She laughs.

"But, Nani, I want to dance with you!" I say.

She pretends to protest, but when she stands up, there's a bounce in her step.

The four of us—Shilpa, Dinesh, Nani, and me—push past the outer ring of people and form our own group toward the center of the dance floor.

Nani's eyes are twinkling as our sticks meet, and I suddenly remember Mr. Markham's question from history earlier today.

"What are some factors that drive immigration to the United States?"

My stick crosses Nani's. I wonder how she must feel seeing all of us dancing to celebrate Navratri. Here. In Maple Grove. This community that she and my grandfather helped to build.

I know she and Nana came here to go to graduate school. And for opportunity.

But I have a feeling they also came here for everyday life. And all the things that go with that. Like friendships, and families, and watching all of us grow up.

I spin past Nani, and my stick hits Dinesh's. I smile, and he grins back.

Now I'm facing Shilpa. I raise both my sticks up to meet hers. Behind her I can see the framed painting of Durga. Shilpa spins her dandiya over her head, and for a second—in her red chaniya choli, which almost matches the red of Durga's sari—her dandiya looks just like Durga's sword.

I laugh softly.

It's not like Shilpa's ever going to ride a lion. Obviously.

But after tonight, I know that when I need her, she'll always be there.

To protect me.

Our sticks meet again, and I nod at her.

I let her know that I'll always be there for her, too.

WEDDING BLUES

by Aisha Saeed

I LOOK AROUND THE CROWDED SPACE I'M STANDING in and do a quick double take. I came to the community center just last week for my chess tournament, but today the main hall has been transformed. The air is filled with the yummy scent of spicy cholay, savory kebabs, and crispy samosas. Upbeat Bollywood music filters in through overhead speakers. Twinkle lights drape the windows. Handmade rugs from my living and dining rooms are unrolled and spread across the laminate flooring right before an enormous stage pushed up against the far wall across from me. It's got a backdrop of red and orange curtains with roses creating an arch over two people who are sitting on a sofa and smiling from ear to ear.

Seeing them, my chest tightens. Quickly, I look away. Mom picked me up from my chess club meeting at school an hour ago, and the hall is already packed. I recognize a few friends by a back window. Two-year-old Rayan's crying wafts over to me from somewhere in the distance—it's impossible to miss his voice, he's a VIP at all desi events (VIP meaning Very Irritating Person). Other than them, I don't recognize a lot of people here.

I do know the two people up on that stage, though. One of them—the one with a sparkle in her eye, her black hair swept up, and grinning from ear to ear—is Khala Shahin, my aunt. The man sitting next to my aunt with brown buzz-cut hair in the white kurta is Brian—or I guess Uncle Brian soon—aka the person taking my aunt away from me. Tomorrow, once they both say "I do" at the wedding, Khala is moving four thousand miles away, across the ocean to a town called Kisumu in Kenya.

"Maha." There's a tap on my shoulder. My mother's head is cocked a little to the side. "We're not pouting again, are we?"

"I'm not pouting." I cross my arms. "There's too many people here. You said it was going to be a small mehndi, but I can't even find a place to sit."

I'm not exaggerating! Not only have the aunties and uncles occupied all the folding chairs that frame the dance floor, they've claimed the dinner seating in the back with purses and scarves to mark the tables as "taken."

"This is a smaller group than the nikkah tomorrow." My mom laughs. "Now come on, sweetie. At least try to look like you're having fun?"

"But I'm not having fun. Why am I supposed to be thrilled she's moving to another continent?"

My mother squeezes her eyes shut for a second. "I know this is hard for you. I'm sad she's leaving, too. The eight years we had with her were very special. But this is a happy moment. She's found someone she loves, and we should be excited for her."

I shift my feet but say nothing. After my parents got divorced, Khala moved all the way from California to New Jersey to live with us when I was three years old. She was there for us and took care of me while my mom finished up residency. All I know is Khala picking me up from school, taking me to the park, playing basketball with me. She's the best at origami, and she's the one who usually tucks me into bed since my mother has so many overnight shifts. She also made the best voices when she read me stories. (My best friend, Rahma, says I'm too old for read-alouds—but she doesn't have my khala reading to her, so she doesn't know what she's missing out on.)

"I'm fine with her getting married. Not that it matters what I think." I shrug. "But she really has to go that far away?"

"It's only two years. They'll be back before you know it."

I shoot her a side-eye at this. She keeps saying that! Brian is a fancy scientist for the government, and he's joining a project in Kenya for work. They promise they'll be back when he finishes up, but even if that's true, two years isn't two days, or weeks, or even months. In two years, I'll go from eleven to thirteen years old! Khala will miss most of my middle school life, which, from what I've heard, is when you need the most support.

Don't get me wrong. I like Brian okay enough. I guess. He's come to my last two soccer games (though he's one of those super loud cringe people cheering in the crowd), and he's a big fan of Studio Ghibli movies like me. I can't point to one thing exactly that I don't like about him, except, if I'm being honest, he's trying a little too hard? Does he *really* think cookies and cream is the best flavor, or is he just saying that because my aunt told him it was my favorite flavor? And either way, it doesn't really matter, because all I see when I look at him up there on the stage smiling and laughing with my aunt is that as nice as he might be, he's the person who came along and ruined everything.

"You look so pretty." My mother traces a hand along my shimmery blouse. "Khala really picked a nice outfit, didn't she?"

"Why did she get me a blue lengha?" I look down at the sky blue skirt. I loved it when I first got it—it's soft and lacy with a chiffon scarf draped across my shoulders. But now that I'm here, it's obvious that I'm completely out of place. Everyone is dressed in bright and bold colors. Yellows, reds, bright oranges. Everyone except me.

"Honey." My mother's voice gets firmer. "You have got to stop complaining. The DJ is late, the caterers are short-staffed, and Rayan just got into the appetizers and nearly toppled the whole table. I have a lot of fires to put out. I need you to try and be a big girl and not sulk."

"Fine," I tell her. I grab a juice box from my bookbag. "I'll sit in the back. That way my *bad* mood won't bother anyone."

My mother frowns, but then suddenly, she brightens. "I have an idea!"

Uh-oh. I do not like the sound of that. Before I can say anything, she's got me by the wrist and is walking me toward the back of the hall. She swings open a brown door I've never noticed before and pulls me into what looks like . . . a gigantic closet?

I tuck my juice box back in my bag and look at the brooms hanging on hooks on the far wall. The dustpan on the ground. Did I annoy my mom so much she's banishing me to the closet?

But we're not the only ones here. There are four older girls in the back corner I know from the masjid, practicing a dance. Tinny-sounding desi music wafts over from one of their phones. And on the other side, I see an assortment of colorful plates and brown mehndi in the center of each. There are two girls sprinkling roses over them and tucking in candles. When I realize who they are, my stomach drops.

Those are my cousins. I knew they'd flown in a little while earlier, but I hadn't seen them until now.

I grip my mom's hand tightly. They're my mom's older sister's kids, and they live on the other side of the country in San Francisco, California. I haven't seen them since last year, when...I shake my head. I don't want to think about that. But before I can protest or ask her what she's doing, my mother marches over to them, dragging me along with her.

"Laila! Roohi!" She smiles. "You've barely landed and you're already at work! Those plates are coming along beautifully. Shahin is going to love this. I'm sure you girls could use a hand, couldn't you?"

Laila and I are two days apart, and Roohi's fifteen. They're wearing matching orange shalwar kameez with glittery reflective beads along the edges. They smile at my mother and give her a hug. When they see me, their mouths press into identical thin lines. They don't even say hello. My heart deflates. Looks like they haven't forgotten what happened last year, either.

My mom grins and pushes me toward them. "Great! This gives you girls a chance to catch up, too!" She pats my back and looks meaningfully at me. "I think that would be nice, especially after all this time, don't you all think so?"

"Mom!" I turn toward her, but she's out before I can say anything. Now I'm here, in an oversized closet, with a bunch of people I barely know or people who wish they didn't know me at all.

I glance at my cousins and fidget with the hem of my blouse. I feel like a volcano about to erupt. I can't believe this! My mother knows how bad things are between me and my cousins. She keeps saying what happened last year wasn't a big deal. She even said that again today after she picked me up from school. But she doesn't get it. To adults, everything *they* go through is the end of the world, but everything someone my age goes through is "not a big deal at all."

There are plates stacked next to my cousins, ready to decorate, and I see at least ten more that probably need to be put together. I should help them. But I can't move. And let's be real, they don't look like they want me to join them one bit.

They say nothing for a few seconds while I stand there awkwardly, but Roohi finally sighs. "If you want to help, grab a plate."

I inch toward them and pick one up. I settle down as far away as possible.

"Fill the plate with mehndi," Roohi tells me. "Laila will add the rose petals, and I'll add in the candle."

We get to work. Quietly we make an assembly line and get the plates put together. I'm glad I can help them out, and the plates look so pretty, but the silence? It really hurts.

This is what happened: Last summer my mom and I visited Roohi and Laila for two weeks like we do each summer. We saw redwoods, hiked through pretty green forests, and picnicked at Dolores Park. On our last day, we'd been at Lands End dipping our toes in the ocean and piling smooth pebbles atop one another on the beach. I was the one who begged for a detour to Fisherman's Wharf and convinced my mom to buy us candies from the fancy chocolate store that had a line out the door. When we got home, Roohi reminded me we weren't allowed to eat in the bedroom, so I *didn't*! But I forgot about the caramel square sample the employees at the chocolate store had handed out. The one I'd stuck in my back pocket.

We were lounging in their room, finishing up the latest round of *Mario Kart*, and when I got up, I heard a loud gasp from my cousins. I had no idea what happened at first, but then I saw it: the white plush fuzzy chair I was sitting on, the brand-new one they'd saved up to buy. It was coated with gooey melted chocolate and caramel.

"Maha!" Roohi had screeched so loud, both our mothers came running in. "It's ruined!"

As my mother googled and my aunt sprayed and scrubbed every fabric cleaner in the house on the chair, I watched as Laila's and Roohi's eyes grew wet with tears. Roohi shook her head at me, her cheeks flushed with anger. I tried to apologize, but my words got stuck in my mouth. That's something that happens when I feel really bad. In that moment, I became one of the redwood trees we'd seen earlier in the week. Silent and rooted to the spot. My heart beat so loudly I could hear it in my head as everyone frantically tried to fix a problem I had made. It was all my fault. The chair was ruined. I was the one who ruined it.

Even now the memory stings.

After that, I holed up in my mom's guest room, and we flew out the next day, as planned. Now, my cousins look warily at me as they pick up empty trays to decorate. The awkwardness is growing and growing. I should say something. The silence is getting more painful than trying to actually talk to them.

"The plates look really nice." I clear my throat.

"Yeah." Roohi glances at her sister and then at me. "They're taking longer than we realized."

"We pulled apart the roses before you got here," Laila says. "My fingers were stained red."

Stained.

At the word, Roohi looks at me and then quickly down at her plate. Nope, they have definitely not forgotten.

I pour the mehndi and pack it onto the plate in

a neat circle like they've done. I hand it to Laila to sprinkle rose petals and shake some glitter on top and watch as Roohi sets in the candle. We've got only one more to go and then we're done. Then I'm getting out of here back to the corner with my juice box where I will hang out for the rest of this party.

As we finish up the last one, the door swings open.

I grimace when I see who it is. Rayan.

Two weeks ago, he'd ripped open half the gifts at Khala's bridal shower. He nearly tipped over the cake at the mayoun last weekend. Didn't my mom just say he'd almost toppled the appetizer table? And now, it appears, he's sidestepped his mom. Again. Rayan isn't looking like a VIP right now; he's in happy mode, which is almost just as scary. He squeals and looks around the space, and then, seeing our plates, his eyes brighten. He walks toward us, stomping his feet, shifting from side to side, like he's Frankenstein.

"Oh no," Roohi says under her breath.

"I got it," Laila says quickly. She moves toward him, but he ducks and she misses his grasp. Rayan is giggling and moving even faster now. He'll be here in five seconds or less.

I look around; there are way too many plates to move them out in time. Even if we gather up some, he'll end up stomping on others. I wince at the thought of all this work going to waste and a toddler with henna-bottomed feet stomping about the hall and onto our handmade rugs.

I run to scoop him up and—success! But now he's wiggling and squirming so much it's like carrying a wet noodle. His face is turning red like a tomato, and I'm afraid I'm going to drop him. Just then, my eyes widen. I know what to do.

"Juice!" I exclaim. I set him on the ground and dig into my bag and pull out the cherry juice box I'd brought along with me from home.

Rayan pauses and looks at what I'm holding. He sees the little white straw, and his eyes widen.

"Jooooos!" he shouts out.

Slowly, he moves toward me. With each step, I take my own step back. It's like he's a horse and the juice box is a carrot, and slowly I walk him toward the door. I push my back against it, and it opens. Once we're safely outside, I scoop him up, give him the juice, and walk him over to his mother.

"Well, that was pretty cool," Roohi says when I return.

"Yeah." Laila nods. "I thought for sure it'd all be ruined."

"Rayan is sweet but a little off-the-wall," I tell them. "Luckily, I had a treat."

"You saved the day." Roohi grins. "Thanks."

Seeing her smile, the words come tumbling out of me.

"I'm so sorry about your chair." My voice trembles. "I know the rules said we couldn't be in the bedrooms with food, and I forgot I had it in my back pocket. But it's no excuse. I ruined your chair. I've been saving up all my birthday money and Eid money so I can buy you a new one, but it's not enough yet."

I finish speaking and draw a shaky breath. I've been waiting to say this for so long. But...will they forgive me?

"It happened last year," Roohi says. "I'm over it."

"But you both still *look* upset," I say.

Laila glances at Roohi and then at me. "You never apologized, Maha. You just stood there and then you went to your mom's room and never came out. Then you left for Jersey. You didn't even say goodbye."

Tears fill my eyes. "I felt so bad, I didn't know what to say. You yelled so loud and I don't blame you—I'd be mad, too. I... I wanted to say goodbye, but I felt so guilty. I didn't think you'd want to see me after that. But I am sorry. I am so, so sorry. I don't want you both to hate me. I'm already losing my aunt, and I don't want to lose more people."

In an instant, Roohi is next to me. Her arm around my shoulder.

"You don't lose your cousins because you have a serious chocolate habit, Maha. And you're not losing Khala. You're gaining a khaloo."

"They're moving to Kenya."

"And we're going to visit them," Laila says. "I heard our moms talking about it on the phone a few weeks ago."

I look at her carefully. I wonder if she's just saying that to make me feel better, but she's smiling and looks like the Laila I've always known.

"Maybe we can do a safari," she adds.

That does sound fun, I think. But...

"I was seven when Khala Shahin moved away from San Francisco to be with you and your mom," Roohi says. "It was hard. She's so fun and tells the best stories. I missed her so much. I know what you're going through."

I'd forgotten about that. Khala had picked up her life and moved it for me all those years ago. Roohi really does understand.

"Luckily, you can still video chat with her every day if you want," Roohi continues. "It's not like she's moving to Mars. I still chat with her a few times a week. And she will be back. It's a long time, I know. But she'll return eventually."

"And also?" Laila adds. "She's really happy. We want her to be happy, right?"

I think about what they are saying. They're right. It doesn't change that I'm sad about this.

But I *do* want my aunt to be happy. She's always putting my drawings on the fridge to ooh and aah over them. She's always with my mom in the front row of any musical I'm part of. She's always happy for my happiness. She moved all the way here all those years ago for me. And if Brian makes her happy, then I should be happy about that. I *am* happy that she's happy.

"And did you know Uncle Brian makes homemade ice cream?" Laila says. "When they came to visit us a few months ago, he made us the best cookies and cream ice cream we ever had!"

"Really?" I smile at this. So, he really does like that flavor. I think about how goofy he gets at my soccer games: he waves both his hands in the air and jumps up and down next to my aunt if I score a goal. It's so dorky, and when everyone looks around to see which of us he belongs to, I pretend I've never seen him before in my life. But even though it's a little embarrassing, he's trying. Maybe I should start trying, too. Maybe this isn't the subtraction problem I've been thinking it is with Khala leaving us. Maybe it's a plus because Brian is joining us.

"Are we ready?" My mom pokes her head in.

"Yes," I tell her. "We are."

A stream of kids from the community come pouring in. We hand them each a plate, giving them advice on how to hold them and reminding them to walk carefully. Mom lights all the candles and then gently ushers the three of us to the front to lead the procession.

"And, girls," my mother says with a big smile. "Don't forget before you leave the stage: Send a bit of sweetness to the bride and groom."

"Really?" Roohi's eyes widen. "We can feed them sweets, too? I thought only adults got to do that."

"Not tonight," my mother says.

"I hope there's laddoos!" Laila grins.

"There's some yellow laddoos and a few other sweets to choose from." But then Mom leans in conspiratorially. "But they're about to eat approximately three hundred of those, so I put unwrapped Dove chocolates on a special plate to the left of all the other sweets. Only letting select folks know about that."

Music fills the room as we step outside and through the open dance square. My stomach fills with butterflies as all the people sitting on folding chairs watch us. I'm not sure I've ever had this many eyes on me. I blink against the brightness that suddenly flashes. The photographer—she's in all black, walking backward and taking photos every step of the way. Of the procession. Of me. Something like this would normally make me want to hide out forever, but I feel less nervous with Roohi and Laila by my side.

We lead the kids to the rugs and set down the candles and plates carefully. The people in the audience clap, and everything we set down glows in unison. I feel a glow in my own heart seeing all our hard work so pretty and on display like this.

I look up at my aunt. She smiles at me and my cousins. Then she gestures for us to join her. We hop up the two steps and stand by the trays of sweets set out to feed the bride and groom: a bit of sweetness as they begin their journey together. The line of aunties is growing behind us. They're getting ready to congratulate them, put henna on their hands, and stuff sweets in their mouths. I can't help but smile a little because I get to be the very first person.

"Chocolate!" Khala's eyes brighten as I kneel by the secret plate and pick one up. I feed her one, then feed Brian the other square.

"Yum!" Brian closes his eyes and smiles really big. "I could get used to this."

"Well, you're about to get fed a lot of dessert," my aunt tells him. "You might be off sugar for the rest of your life after tonight."

Before I can step off the stage, Khala takes my hands and holds them tight.

"These plates look gorgeous. And so do you."

"Thanks." I hesitate and then add, "The lengha is pretty, but it's blue. It's different from what everyone else is wearing."

"That's why I got it for you. Blue is your favorite color, right? I wanted you to stand out and feel special in your favorite color."

I give my aunt a big hug, and she hugs me back just as tightly.

"I'm going to miss you," I tell her.

"You too, kiddo," she says. "So much. But I'm only leaving the house. I'm not leaving you. You're stuck with me for life."

"That goes for me, too," Brian—Uncle Brian—adds with a wink. "Starting tomorrow, it'll be official!"

I'm about to roll my eyes, but I pause and look at him again, his big smile crinkling his eyes. And today, instead of furrowing my brow, I smile back at him.

I hop down the stairs and join my cousins at the side of the stage. The girls who'd been practicing a dance are starting up their song. We watch them twirl and spin in unison. I feel a little lighter as I watch them.

No matter what happens, no matter where she goes, she'll always be my khala.

SMILE NUMBER SEVEN

by Mitali Perkins

"PON! STOP! PON! STOP!"

I'm shouting at peak volume, words cannonballing out between gasps. This behavior is unusual for a person known at my middle school as "The Mute," but it's necessary. Our golden retriever is bounding across a parking lot, leash trailing, and I'm tearing after him.

Someone grabs the leash right before Pon disappears through an open door. I'm panting as I reach them. It's a kid from school—Alok—and his mouth falls open as he recognizes me. Pon is drooling on his tennis shoes.

Alok hands me the leash. "Wow. Never heard you yell like that before, Steven. Didn't know you had it in you. And what a great dog!"

I nod my thanks. *And what a bad dog*, I think, shooting Pon a stern look. He hangs his head.

"Didn't know you could run that fast, either. Play any basketball?" Alok dribbles a few times, waiting for me to answer.

I catch sight of a few other kids shooting baskets on a court at the end of the parking lot. Basketball? Me? Is he kidding? Like most of the other boys in our school, even some sixth graders, Alok's a good two inches taller than me and probably ten pounds heavier. I shake my head no.

"You should try it sometime. It's the best sport ever."

Agree to disagree, I think. Alok gives Pon a last

pat and shakes the drool off his sneakers. Then he dribbles off to join his friends.

Where *are* we, anyway? I look around and spot a sign in front of the building: MAPLE GROVE COMMUNITY CENTER. The door Pon almost ran through is propped open, and a delicious aroma of rice comes wafting out to where we're standing. It smells amazing. No wonder my ever-hungry dog wanted to go in. We both move closer to the door. Clutching Pon's leash tightly, I inhale another whiff of the food and listen for a moment to the sounds of conversation and laughter and music coming from inside.

"Bù hǎo yì si," says a voice behind me.

I spin. Behind me is the new girl at school—Chen Li. Behind her is a man carrying two badminton rackets. Must be her father, I think, because she sure looks like him. Behind *him* are five more kids from our school accompanied by men who look like *their* fathers, each carrying two badminton rackets.

I back away from the door and pull Pon with

me. Before Chen leads the way in, she gives Pon a pat and then flashes me a smile—*that* smile.

Pon looks up at me. I look down at him. He's drooling. I might be, too. It's October and this makes Smile Number Six, but who's counting? Well, I am. I most definitely am. With every smile, my desire to know the person behind the smiles keeps growing. Which is weird, because I've been a loner my whole life, mostly thanks to my apraxia—or "motor speech disorder," as my special education file defines it. Before Chen Li showed up, I'd *never* wanted to get to know any girl better. But how do two people become friends when one can't speak much English and the other can't speak much at all?

A badminton player's foot dislodges the doorstop and the door swings closed once they're all inside. I spot a flyer posted on the door and move closer to read it. "Parent-Child Badminton Club. Saturdays. 4 p.m. Meet in the gym. Coordinator: Coach Vic."

So *that's* where they're going. Does this mean

Chen will be coming to the Maple Grove Community Center every Saturday? To play *badminton*, of all things? I'm having a mini mind explosion right now, because badminton—*not* basketball—is the best sport ever. And one I can actually play. My grandfather always says a badminton court is a superb place to get to know the true nature of a person. I snap a picture of the flyer with my phone.

As Pon and I head home, I take an inventory of my Chen Li Smile Collection. Number One came on her first day of school, when Jeff Holmes—whose mean streak takes over when he's bored—edged the front of his desk against the back of her chair, pinning her long silky hair. I knuckled him on the shoulder and scowled, staying in place until he shrugged and inched his desk back. Chen turned her head slightly and flashed Number One at me. I floated back to my seat.

Number Two arrived after I picked up her pen and handed it to her.

Number Three turned up after I wrote Mr. Murphy a note and he read it aloud—in front of the entire science class—to "commend my character." I was late because I'd been leading a lost sixth grader to the right classroom. It was mortifying to stand there in front of all those eyes, but Chen's smile made it worth the effort.

Number Four lit up her face as we passed each other in the hallway.

Number Five was brilliant. Chen put her head in her arms after some idiots snickered at something she'd said in English. She must have used a British translator app on her phone because she'd raised her hand and said, "I need loo, please." What's funny about that? Nothing. I scribbled the words "I need to go to the bathroom" on a slip of paper and tucked it under her elbow. She lifted her head, read the note, turned to find me, and *boom*—Number Five sparkled my way. Then she raised her hand and said the phrase perfectly.

Today, of course, was Number Six. And if all goes according to my new plan, Number Seven will dazzle me on a badminton court at Maple Grove Community Center.

Pon and I are almost home. Our block is lined with small ranch houses with front porches and pocket-sized lawns or gardens. As usual, on a sunny fall Saturday afternoon, most of the porches are occupied. Three toddlers are making one huge leaf pile, a neighbor is sweeping leaves off his porch, another is straightening pillows on her outdoor furniture, and the elderly woman next door is sipping tea, watching gold and orange leaves drift down from the maple trees lining the street. This is supposed to be a friendly neighborhood. For years, people invited us to meals or gatherings, but they gave up after Amma's repeated refusals.

Pon leads me up the three stairs to our leaf-covered porch and past the two rocking chairs my grandparents gave us. They're covered with leaves, too. Amma and I never sit in them. Nobody does.

Inside the living room, my mother's asleep with the Golf Channel on mute. Amma's wiry, short, and dark-skinned, like me, and because we look alike, we don't get questions from strangers about adoption. The question we do get, though, again and again, is about my nonexistent father. Amma usually handles that one: "Steven doesn't have a dad." Period. The way she says it shuts them up.

After feeding Pon, I put in an order for Chinese takeout. Amma wakes with a jolt when the delivery guy rings the doorbell. "We've sure been having a lot of Chinese lately," she says, taking stock of the small white boxes I'm setting out on the kitchen island.

I shrug and dish up plates of rice and orange chicken and we sit side by side on our usual stools. As we eat, my eyes keep darting her way.

Amma sighs. "What's on your mind, Stevie?" she asks. Then she waits and chews.

"Badminton." Words come easier when I'm with Amma or my grandparents. Almost everyone else on the planet isn't as patient with my apraxia.

"Badminton? Why? It's not Sunday."

Amma used to compete in college in Kerala, and we practice during our Sunday visits to my grandparents. She's spent a lot of time teaching me how to hit clears, smashes, drives, and drops.

Appachan used to play too, which made it more fun, but he had to stop a few weeks ago when he twisted his ankle.

I swallow my bite of orange chicken and show Amma the picture of the flyer on my phone. She takes one look and shakes her head. "No way. I'll bet it's a bunch of Indians. You know how I feel about being around *them*."

My turn to sigh. I do know. She's said plenty about the "gossip and shaming" she endured from *them* as a woman who (1) decided to stay single and (2) adopted and is raising a "special-needs" kid on her own. During my baptism at the Immanuel Church of South India Congregation where my grandparents attend, she overheard the vicar saying he agreed to offer me the sacrament even though my mother was "acting outside the will of the Lord to raise a fatherless boy." Amma took me up in her arms, stormed out, and never returned. Ever since then, apart from seeing my grandparents, we've both been loners.

But not for long. I'm not giving up on my plan.

If I want to get to know Chen, it won't happen at school, where words—chattered and shouted and cursed and complimented—swirl around us like a cyclone. Badminton at the community center might be my only chance, and somehow, I'll have to change Amma's mind. This means a consult with my grandfather. Appachan's the only person on earth my mother turns to for advice, which isn't often.

On Sunday morning, we leave Pon to destroy a chew toy inside his crate and walk the ten blocks to my grandparents' house as usual. We let ourselves in because they're still at church. Ammachi has left potatoes, carrots, and eggplant for sambar on the kitchen counter. While I chop those, Amma dices onions, garlic, and ginger and mixes spices for a red fish curry. By the time my grandparents return—silvery-haired, petite Ammachi smiling, decked out in a blue-and-gold sari, and tall, thin Appachan humming a hymn, wearing a starched white shirt, navy suit, and red tie—everything's ready.

The four of us laugh and talk and eat until Ammachi's eyes dart in Amma's direction. I catch Appachan raising his eyebrows to telegraph a "don't do it" warning, but Ammachi ignores him, takes a deep breath, and launches into forbidden territory. "Mariam, darling, you and Steven simply must meet the new vicar. You'd really like—"

She stops mid-sentence because Amma's face has transformed into a NO TRESPASSING sign. My mother picks up her glass of water, drains it in one swallow, and bangs it back down on the table. Not hard enough to break, but with just enough force to make her point.

We keep eating, this time in silence. I'm a bit surprised that Ammachi brought up the subject of church. My grandparents stopped inviting us to join them long ago, but I know they still wish we would go with them. Appachan left his diary open one day, and I saw his prayer in bold, black printing: "Please, God, restore my dear Mariam and Steven back into community. Bring them back to church in your timing, Lord."

After lunch, Ammachi disappears for her afternoon nap, and we head to the backyard, where Appachan watches Amma and me play badminton. My grandfather's taken off his suit jacket and rolled up his shirtsleeves. He's clutching an imaginary racket as if he's playing along, and his hand and wrist flick each time the shuttlecock comes my way. Amma beats me as usual, but our scores are closer these days, and we're both drenched in sweat at the end of an hour, not just me. She goes inside to shower, and I join Appachan on the deck. This is my chance to get his advice.

"You're improving," he tells me. "You'd crush me if I were still playing."

I pull out my phone and show him the flyer.

His eyebrows shoot up so high on his bald head that for a second it looks as if he's grown some hair. "Oh! Well! Steven, this is a surprise. I actually know the person who's in charge of that activity. Has your mother agreed to join you?"

Frowning, I figure-eight my head in an Indian no.

"Ah. Let me handle her, shall I?" He gives me a keen look. "Were any of the other players your age accompanied by a mother?"

Negative head twist again.

"Perfect."

When Amma comes out, her curly hair wet and smelling of sandalwood soap, it's my turn to shower, so I go inside. But, of course, I stay in the living room near the open window to eavesdrop.

Appachan starts with an announcement. "I shall be joining Stevie on Saturdays at Maple Grove Community Center's Badminton Club."

"What? No! You can't. Your ankle's still recovering."

"Sport is the perfect venue for forming a friendship, and Stevie needs friends. But since he is a fatherless child, I shall have to accompany him."

Oooh, good one, Appachan.

"How can you say that, Appa?" my mother asks. I flinch, because her tone sounds hurt instead of angry. "You know how much that phrase bothers me."

They're quiet for a bit.

"Besides, you're Stevie's *grandfather*," Amma says. "The flyer said *Parent*-Child, if I remember right."

Good. Now she sounds more like her fighting self.

Appachan's voice stays kind and steady. "Ah, yes, it did, didn't it? Well, Stevie told me that the other children all had fathers with them. He'd be the only one with a mother if you go."

"Well, I'm not going. And neither is Stevie."

"The doctor said I'll be back on my feet in two weeks' time," Appachan says. "If you don't accompany Stevie to this club before then, I shall."

More silence.

Then: "Let's go, Steven! You can shower at home." Amma stalks out of the house without the usual hugs and kisses and waits on the sidewalk.

"Take along our two finest rackets, Stevie," Appachan tells me.

Calling out a quick goodbye to Ammachi, I race out to the backyard and grab the rackets.

But when I come out the front door holding them, Amma's signature scowl deepens.

Appachan puts his arms around me and whispers, "She'll join you, I'm sure of it."

But he's wrong. On Saturday at three, Amma takes Pon for a walk and they aren't back by three forty-five, so I head to the community center on my own. I don't take a racket because I'm not sure what I'm going to do. Maybe I'll go inside the gym. Maybe I won't.

It's 4:10 by the time I get there, and the door isn't propped open today. I stand on the sidewalk near the entrance, trying to gather my courage to go inside. Alok approaches, but this time he has a fancy kurta in a dry cleaner's plastic bag slung over his arm even though he's still toting a basketball.

"You coming to the Navratri celebration, Steven?" Alok asks. "It's the last night."

I shake my head no. I have no idea what he's talking about. His buddies are around him now, and he holds the door open and waits, so there's nothing else to do but follow them inside. We walk down a hallway full of sunlight pouring through a glass ceiling that's arching above our heads. Alok and his friends enter a big room on the right, which is full of sitar music, people setting up tables, laughter and talking, and more fantastic food smells. A sign on the wall near the open door reads BANQUET ROOM.

Across the hall is a closed door with a long, narrow glass panel above the handle. A sign nearby reads GYMNASIUM. I walk over. A handwritten sign is posted on the door. "Parent-Child Badminton Club. Please come in."

It's easy to see through the glass. Chen is on the far side of the gym. Her ponytail swirls around as she dives for the shuttlecock when it's short and dashes back to cover a lob. Her father is on the court with her, and after he misses an easy shot, he mimics his own awkward movements and everyone laughs.

From the hall, I count five badminton courts and twenty players. The other players my age are a mix of girls and boys, but their parent partners are men. All of them seem to know the basics. A few aren't quite as good as Amma and me, but almost. A short woman who looks fit and strong is wandering the floor, holding a clipboard and watching the games.

I put my hand on the door handle. *Go in*, I tell myself. But I don't. Twenty players. Twenty heads. Forty eyes will stare when player number 21, the only one without a parent, enters the room.

I can't do it.

I can't walk in there.

But I also can't make myself leave.

Because oh, how I want to play badminton.

And oh, how I want to play badminton with Chen Li.

I'm still trying to make myself open the door when someone yells behind me, "LOOK OUT!"

I let go of the door handle and spin, just in time for a hurtling basketball to smash against my face.

Hard.

Blood gushes from my nostrils.

I hate the sight of blood, especially my own.

And now there's so much of it.

The hall spins.

Faces blur around me.

Bam! I'm down for the count.

When my eyes flutter open, a lady in white and gold is kneeling beside me. Am I in heaven? But she can't be an angel because she's trying to smother me. I start to push her hand away but then realize that she's using her scarf to stop the bleeding.

"Press it against your nose," she says, handing me the entire scarf. "I'm a doctor; I've had a look at your face while you were out. Your nose isn't broken. I don't think you hit your head—your elbows took your fall."

I'm in the hallway, flat on my back on the floor. Sunlight coming through the glass ceiling dazzles my eyes, so I squint to see the circle of brown faces gazing down at me. Some are old, some are Amma's age, and some look like teenagers, but all of them share the same expression—what is that, anyway? Concern? Care? My head is still spinning. For one weird moment, it feels as if the light is coming from these faces instead of from above them.

"Come, we'll drive you home," the woman is saying. "Amit, go and get the car, please. Boys, help your friend."

Alok and one of his friends manage to pull me to my feet, but I still feel woozy. The front of the doctor's white and gold shalwar kameez is covered with blood.

My blood.

I stagger.

"Here, Steven, lean on me," Alok says. "I'm so sorry about the basketball! We got here early, so Rohit and I were going to shoot around with our friends while everyone set up." He looks over his shoulder at the other kids. "At least this time the flying basketball wasn't my fault! Come on, we'll take you to Uncle Amit's car. Put an arm around each of us."

And so I do. Slowly, in lockstep, me on tiptoes and both of them slouching down, they lead me out to the parking lot, where a sparkling white Mercedes is waiting. Alok and his friend ease me into the back seat and say goodbye. The seats are pearly, too. Does everything these people own have to be so white? But none of it stays like that because my nose has started bleeding again. Even though I'm pressing the scarf against my face, my blood dribbles across the entire back seat in a pattern of red dots.

The doctor climbs into the passenger seat and turns around. "Don't worry about the car; we'll clean it up. Someone at the community center called your mother to tell her we're coming."

How did they get Amma's number? A family with a kid at my school, maybe? I'm sure she's freaking out with worry. It doesn't take long to get home. Before the Mercedes pulls to a stop, my mother comes bursting out of the door, Pon bounding behind her. The doctor quickly steps out of the car to meet Amma.

I nod my thanks to the driver and slowly climb out of the back seat. Pon leaps up and puts his paws on my shoulders. He has his tongue ready in case I need him to clean off the blood. I don't. I push him down.

"Go wait on the porch, Steven," Amma says, grabbing Pon. "Can someone tell me what happened?"

I trudge to our front porch, brush away the leaves on one of the rocking chairs, and take a seat. The chair creaks in protest, as if it's surprised by the weight of an actual body.

On the sidewalk, Amma is repeating words like "nine-one-one" and "so much blood," but the woman's calm voice is speaking, too. I rock back and forth, pressing the scarf, which is more red than white by now, against my nose. The blood seems to be stopping. Finally.

After a while, the woman climbs back into the Mercedes and Amma joins me. "Lucky you fainted in front of a doctor," she says, brushing the leaves off the other chair and sitting down. "She says you'll be fine."

Amma's chair joins mine, squeaking in shock.

Pon makes himself comfortable on a pile of leaves. I show my mother the stained scarf.

"I'll have it laundered," she says. "We'll get it back to her somehow. I'm so grateful they took care of you, Stevie."

Her voice breaks when she says my name; she isn't looking at me, but suddenly I notice the tears on her cheeks. Tears? Amma? I can't remember the last time she cried. I reach over and take her hand. She doesn't pull away.

We rock in silence, holding hands. The porches on our street are full of curious people pretending not to watch us. Pon gets up, puts his head on my lap, and looks up at me. *Good dog*, I think, remembering how he led me to Maple Grove Community Center. *Best dog ever.*

I remember the concerned faces around me as I lay on my back in the hallway.

I think of how Alok and his friend slouched down to be closer to my height and offered me their shoulders to lean on.

I picture Chen's father getting everyone to laugh by making fun of himself.

Circled. Supported. Connected. That's what I want. That's what I need.

Letting go of Amma's hand, I make my decision. This loner stuff comes to an end right now. At least for me. How my mother decides to respond is up to her. Once again, I pull up the photo of the Badminton Club flyer and show it to her.

Once again, she shakes her head no. "I'm sorry, Stevie. I... can't."

"Appachan," I say.

"He's too old. He'll get hurt again."

I tap my chest and force out the words: "Me, then. Alone."

Amma's quiet, but her chair is rocking hard now. *SQUEEEEAK. CREAAK. SQUEEAK. CREAK.* After a while, she slows it down and sighs. "Okay, Stevie, you win. I'll give it a try next Saturday. Just once. If I hate it, will you quit asking me to join things?"

I drop a kiss on Pon's golden head. No, I think. I won't.

The next day, we skip the visit to my grandparents' house because Amma wants me to rest. On Monday at school, Chen's desk is empty. Mr. Murphy stops me as I'm leaving to tell me she's transferred to the gifted and talented science class. For the rest of the week, I don't run into her in the halls or in the cafeteria. Her entire schedule must have changed. At lunch, though, instead of eating alone like I usually do, Alok calls me over, and I join him and Rohit and a bunch of other kids. Alok adds me to their text thread so I can weigh in on the apps and games they're arguing about. Getting notifications from kids at Maple Grove Middle School is new. But it feels good. Great, in fact. Texting, I can do.

Saturday finally comes, and Amma and I arrive at the community center right at four. After we leave the doctor's laundered, folded scarf at the front desk, we head to the gym. There's no party today, so the hallway is much quieter, and it's cloudy, so there's no sunlight coming through the ceiling. Amma's clutching both of our rackets across her chest so they look like a shield. Her face is stony as she trudges along beside me.

I feel a twinge of guilt, so I decide to give her one last chance to escape when we stop outside the gym door. Turning to face her, I raise my eyebrows.

She shrugs, so I open the door.

I walk in. Amma follows.

Most of the other players are already there. On the far side of the gym, I see Chen drop a shuttlecock as she catches sight of me, but then—she smiles. And, oh, it's another good one this time. It's an amazing one, in fact. Even from here I can see that her entire face is crinkled with delight.

Amma's head swivels from Chen to my huge grin as I reply to Number Seven. "Aha, Stevie," she says, but she keeps her voice low.

It's my turn to shrug, but I can't stop smiling.

The stocky woman I'd seen before comes to greet us. "Mariam? Steven?"

How does she know our names? Amma looks confused, too.

"Your father told me to keep an eye out for the two of you," the woman says. "I'm the newly installed vicar at Immanuel Church of South India Congregation. But I'm known in badminton circles as Coach Vic."

Amma's looking as if someone just smashed *her* in the face with a basketball, so I stretch out my hand.

Coach Vic shakes it and turns back to Amma. "Your parents told me you played badminton back in Trivandrum, Mariam? I did as well. What years were you in college? Maybe we competed against each other."

I nudge Amma with my elbow, and she manages to mutter a reply.

"Well, that's a little before me," says Coach Vic. "In any case, I'm so delighted you're here. You see, I've been thinking and praying about adopting a child from Kerala, and your parents thought you might be able to advise me."

Amma and I exchange a glance. What's that I

see in my mother's eyes? Surprise, yes, but something else, too. Wonder, maybe?

"Are you married?" she asks Coach Vic.

"No. I'm on my own. And if I do adopt, I'll likely be a single parent for life. That's why I want so much to talk this decision over with you. Both of you, in fact."

Amma hands me a racket. "Why don't you come to our house after practice? It's a beautiful afternoon. We can have tea on our porch."

We'll have to drag out another chair, and maybe even a table. I'll get rid of the leaves. It's cloudy and cool, but the sun might break through.

"Sounds delightful," Coach Vic says. "Now get out there and play so I can see if you're both as good as your father claims. Steven, since you already seem to know Chen, why don't you practice with them?"

Clutching one of Appachan's best rackets, I sprint to the far side of the gym, my heart so light it feels like a flying shuttlecock. Smile Number Seven is waiting for me, still going strong.

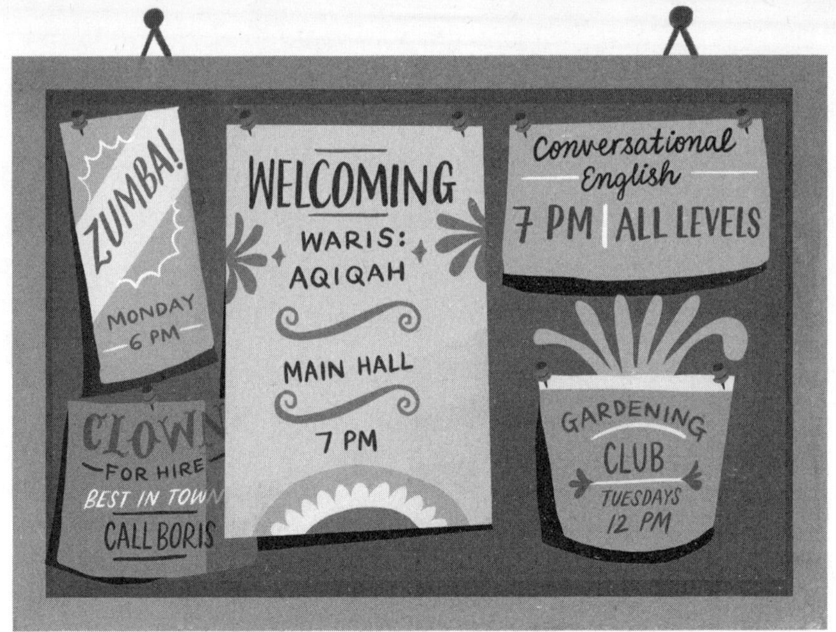

SWEET AND SOUR

by Reem Faruqi

SPLAT!

Khadeejah's eyes crinkle, and she smiles as she waves her spoon at the gloppy kichri that drips off my shirt.

"KHADEEEJAAAAH!" I wail as I start jabbing at my shirt. My once-new shirt, which is now ruined.

Suddenly, the iPad rings. It's Nani.

In one swift movement, I scoop Khadeejah out of her high chair. I balance her, the spoon that is coated in kichri mush, and the iPad all on my hip. I swipe up on the iPad, leaving just one smudgy fingerprint behind. Success!

I love having a tech-savvy grandmother. Right now, Nani's screen moves slightly. She wipes a film of sweat off her forehead. Whenever she walks, she wears her hot pink headphones.

"Assalamalaikum, beti, how are you?"

She adjusts her hijab and looks at me expectantly. I exhale. Hearing Nani's voice makes me feel better, even if she isn't here in real life.

"I'm okay, but Khadeejah just ruined my shirt."

Khadeejah starts to clap, the kind of clapping where only silence comes out because her hands are so squishy.

"I'm sorry...which shirt is it?"

I scan the iPad lower so Nani can see.

"Oye ma! The new one I gave you!" exclaims Nani before making soft tsk-tsk sounds.

I nod glumly. Even though Nani's on a screen, her face invites me to say more. But before I have the chance, Mom comes by and takes the iPad from me. She smells like shampoo and wears her towel on her head.

I wash Khadeejah's hands and try to dab the top half of my shirt, but it looks like I've attacked it with a yellow highlighter. Turmeric is hard to remove, and Mom always adds a generous pinch of the spice in her kichri. I should know. I've been helping Mom feed both of my little sisters for a while now.

Ding!

A message from Nani.

Don't worry about the shirt. I'll show you how to bleach it... I can't wait to see you tomorrow!

My fingers fly as I type.

Thanks. Me too. I wish Khadeejah and Hawwa were much older already!

What I wouldn't give to have a sister I could actually hang out with, not just babysit.

I'm eleven. Khadeejah is two and a half years

old. My other sister, Hawwa, is one. I wonder what life would be like with both my sisters born closer to me in age, or even both of them born in the same decade! Sometimes the age gap just seems way too big.

Ding!

I had the same problem. My brother is ten years younger than me. But we are very close now!

Ding! A photo.

A man I recognize from Nani's photos from her Pakistan trip stands much taller than Nani. They look different, but when I zoom in, I see they have the same wide smiles. I love how Nani's smile starts small but gets big quickly.

My brother Wahab has a granddaughter your age. Amena. I've mentioned her a few times.

Really? Someone my age? That doesn't happen much lol.

She doesn't live here... you haven't met them yet because they recently moved from Pakistan to Atlanta.

Typical!

But they are all coming to the aqiqah. You both

looked alike as babies. There's a photo of you when you went to Pakistan as a baby. I'll find it.

Before bed, I'm setting the alarm on the iPad when... *Ding!*

An image pops up. It's a little grainy. Two babies sitting next to each other. One looks like it's me. We're dressed alike in little pink shalwar kameezes. But Nani's wrong...we just look like babies, nothing alike!

Nothing at all alike, unlike Nani and her brother, with their exact same smiles.

"Watch the girls! I have a call," Mom hollers as she grabs her notepad.

"Okay." I drop my bookbag to the floor. "But I have homework..."

But Mom doesn't hear me and goes upstairs, closing the door firmly behind her.

As I open my math workbook, I notice Hawwa and Khadeejah are digging through my lunch box for snacks without success.

After a few minutes, Mom comes down and starts to heat up some food.

"How was school?" she asks.

I am describing how we are going to get an ice cream party for being the class that volunteers the most when Khadeejah starts crying. My sisters are fighting over crayons. They start out whimpering, but it escalates to screaming and snatching. Mom stops listening to me while she calmly takes away crayons from each kid. Khadeejah pouts.

"Continue..."

But it's too late. I don't continue. My story doesn't matter. Again.

Mom doesn't even notice that I stop talking. Instead, the oven beeps and she exhales before pulling out fish sticks and sweet potato tots from the oven.

Other families eat desi food every day like my Sunday school friends, but Mom says she doesn't have enough time to cook. I think my sisters may be the reason.

Dinner goes mostly okay, but as Mom scoops up Hawwa, she notices that Hawwa has been hiding most of her tots in her high chair. Khadeejah starts to smush them.

"STOP!" I yell, but it's too late. Khadeejah smushes one into Hawwa's hair.

"Oops…" mumbles Mom. "At least this happened before bath time…."

I giggle. Hawwa's hair has orange globs in it. She quickly smushes one into Khadeejah's hair.

"Food fight!" I gasp.

"NO! Bath time!" commands Mom as she lifts each kid up and puts them on her hips and marches them upstairs. Finally, peace.

I peek into the guest room. Mom has somehow managed to clean it up and keep it that way. With Khadeejah and Hawwa around, that doesn't happen much. Mom's put sunflowers in a vase and a packet of salty pistachios on the dresser for Nani.

I glance at my watch and calculate how much time is left until Nani flies in from Detroit today. I ignore my homework, grab Khadeejah and

Hawwa's crayons off the sticky floor, and draw a sign. My fingers fly over the letters. "WELCOME NANI!"

Only a few more hours until Baba and I go to get her. I grab the iPad to sneak in a quick call. Nani's at the airport gate.

"Rahma, how are you?"

"Okay..."

"And the terrible toddlers?" chuckles Nani.

"They were starting a food fight!"

Nani chuckles as I describe Hawwa's hair.

"Listen. How about I put you in touch with Amena?"

I'm not sure. Grown-ups act like just because two people are the same age, you're supposed to magically get along. Would it be awkward to talk to a complete stranger? I have no idea what Amena is like. Then again, this Amena girl is family... technically my second cousin, *and* she isn't a toddler.

Nani reads my thoughts, even through a screen.

"She's family. And she'll feel more welcome at the aqiqah. She's been in Pakistan most of her life, so she'll finally be meeting her American family. My brother, Wahab, is going to be spending a few months in Atlanta with them before flying back to Pakistan again."

"Okay, sure..."

"I'll give you her info when I see you," sings Nani. "See you soon, insha'Allah!"

At the airport, Nani swoops me up in a warm hug. Nani isn't bony like me, but instead soft and rounded. It makes the hug even better.

On the way home, Baba stops at a Pakistani restaurant in downtown Maple Grove to pick up our usual order—Chicken 65, saag paneer, butter chicken, rice, and naan—as a treat for Nani. I clutch the warm takeout containers on my lap and savor the spicy smell as Baba drives home. Even though I'm squished up by big car seats, I listen to Nani's smooth voice tell stories while Baba drives us home.

At home, I get to enjoy a second dinner without my little sisters because Nani's here. Mom has somehow managed to put both Khadeejah and Hawwa to bed and has even changed out of her regular sweatpants that she wears all day into a cheerful yellow shalwar kameez.

Since Khadeejah and Hawwa are asleep, this dinner goes way better than the first one. Plus, there's no one to complain about the food being too spicy. After I'm really full, I help Nani unpack. The aqiqah for my new baby cousin Waris is still two months away, but Nani's here for a quick visit to help Ghazala Khala with him.

"I can't wait for the aqiqah. They're my favorite celebrations because we welcome a new baby to the family!" coos Nani. In *The Lion King*, baby Simba is presented to all the animals. I guess you can say we're presented to all our parents' friends at the community center on our aqiqah. "Look at this little sherwani I bought for him to wear that day. And look, it's extra soft for babies!"

The tiny shalwar kameez is soft and a deep blue color. I rub it against my cheek.

"So, tomorrow I'll be visiting Ghazala Khala

to help her with Waris. Babies are a lot of work," Nani says.

"I know!" I remember when Hawwa and Khadeejah were tiny. They were snuggly but also cranky. For some reason, my sisters were never the quiet babies with cute little cries. They were loud and cried at maghrib, when the sun set, right after Baba came home.

I shudder. Nani chuckles.

"Here. I brought something for you."

"Huh? Note cards? I already got my school supplies, Nani." I flip over the heavy white cards. There are three lines on the card. Weird.

"They're postcards, for you to write letters to Amena."

"Ohhh. Right. I don't really do postcards. Doesn't she have email?"

Nani is usually so tech-savvy. I'm surprised.

"I'm sure she does, but my brother and I loved exchanging postcards when we lived far apart. It would be a nice project for you to get to know each other before the aqiqah. They're blank so you can decorate the front of the cards. Getting old-fashioned mail is fun. You'll see."

"Thanks, Nani." I should be more excited, but school just started, and writing feels like extra work.

"My brother just gave her some postcards, too. Let the exchange begin!" Nani claps. "Think how fun it'll be when you meet for the aqiqah. You'll already know her! Why don't you start writing?"

Nani blinks at me expectantly.

"Fine."

I run to my desk, rummage through my drawers, and find a sparkling blue gel pen and a blunt pencil. As I sharpen the pencil, I think, *I'll just do one postcard to make Nani happy.* I head back to the guest room and start writing.

Hello Amena

I erase "hello."

Assalamalaikum Amena.

What do you say to someone you don't know but who is related to you?

Nani points to the blank square and taps two times with an orange fingernail, stained with mehndi.

"Actually, that's where you write. The lines are for the address."

I sigh as I erase again.

I'm your second cousin.

I'll also be at the aqiqah and heard you're coming.

Do you have any brothers or sisters?

Rahma

Nani peers over my shoulder.

"Why not tell her more? You have space."

I erase for the third time.

I have two sisters. They're very small and very loud. They're two years old and one year old. What about you?

The postcard still looks a smidge blank. I draw hearts around my name in sparkly blue pen.

Nani writes the address on the three lines. "There. Missing anything?"

"A stamp?"

"Yes." She rummages through her suitcase. "Here. Special stamps for postcards."

"Gosh, Nani, what *don't* you have in your suitcase?"

"Tikkuh, tikkuh!" yells Hawwa, who's just walked in and is now trying to grab the stamps.

I groan. Hawwa's escaped from her crib again.

"She thinks they're stickers." I pull the stamps away from her. This makes Hawwa yell louder.

"*Fine*, Hawwa. You can stick my stamp on." I point to the square.

Hawwa sticks the stamp all crooked in the wrong place.

"Moooom! Hawwa's awake!" I holler. Mom has her rubber gloves on, which means she's loading the dishwasher.

Seeing Hawwa out of her crib, Mom's shoulders

droop. “Can you take her back up, Rahma? Baba had to finish some work, and I’ll be there in a few minutes. . . .”

“Sure,” I sigh. I want to read my latest Baby-Sitters Club graphic novel, but it looks like I’ll be reading Llama Llama.

“Back to bed, Hawwa!”

I pick her up and tiptoe into the room that we all share to put Hawwa back in her crib and pray she doesn’t wake Khadeejah. I whisper the words of *Llama Llama Red Pajama* to Hawwa. When I try to skip over a couple of pages, she immediately sits up and makes me read it again. It looks like it’s going to be a long night.

When I pull open the empty mailbox to put my postcard inside, I open and close its door a few times to hear the creaky sound before raising the red metal flag.

Will I really get a postcard back from my cousin? What if she reads my card and doesn’t want to write back? Maybe she’s not into postcards, the way I wasn't, either. Maybe she thinks it's a big waste of time.

When Nani and I go to visit Waris, I lounge on the couch. All he does is sleep and look around without really focusing. Waris is adorable, though, and his cries are not like Khadeejah's or Hawwa's. Ghazala Khala says if I visited at two a.m., that would be a much different story.

Over the next few days, I check the mailbox repeatedly, but nothing. So much for having a cousin, even if it is a second cousin. I don't get anything back. After another empty mailbox, I throw my hands in the air. Sensing my mood, Nani says it's teatime. Instead of making tea quickly like Mom and Baba, she boils tea bags in a pot filled with milk and waits for it to simmer slowly.

Khadeejah and Hawwa are napping, and it's nice to have Nani all to myself. In peace. I hover over the pot to feel the steam hug my palms before reaching for a teacup for Nani.

"Nani, I still haven't gotten anything from Amena!"

"It's called snail mail, not rabbit mail!" answers Nani as she takes a sip of her chai. "Maybe something will come in a few days?"

Two days later, I reach for the mail again. Just bills. And junk mail. Like usual. But then, something small peeks out underneath the envelopes. The handwriting is new. The letters are spaced out and rounded. Is it? It couldn't be. It is!

A postcard!

Dear Rahma,

You're so lucky you have sisters! I have a brother and he always fights with me and leaves his stinky socks all around my room and even in my bed under my pillow as a joke. Gross! What's your favorite color? Mine is purple. What do you do for fun? I like to illustrate and write stories.

Sincerely,

Amena

I flip over the postcard. Wow. Amena can draw! I'd made two loopy hearts. She's drawn swirly roses out of crayon that look 3-D. I can't believe she actually wrote back. She sounds like she's creative and fun to be around. I have a good feeling that we may get along after all. After showing Nani, I rush inside to my desk to write back. I reach for a purple gel pen and write extra small, so everything fits. This time, I write the address in the right spot the first time.

Amena,

I finally got your postcard!! I loved your art. I wish I could draw that well. How old is your brother? That's annoying about the stinky socks. My sisters have stinky diapers.

For fun, I like to swim. But sometimes we don't get to go to the pool because of nap time and then my mom has work. And it's a lot of work, says my mom, to take three kids to the pool when my dad isn't there. So, then it's just weekends. IF we're lucky. They have a lot of stuff, like floats, towels, toys, and sunscreen. Last time my little sister Khadeejah had a tantrum when we didn't have the right towel for her!

I know how to swim, but my sisters don't yet.

I wish my sisters were older. Then I could actually have more fun with them. Instead, it feels like all I do is watch them. My cousins too!

Write back!

Rahma

Dear Rahma,

That's annoying about not getting to swim. Since we moved here, we swim all the time! My brother, Hamzah, likes to do cannonballs into the pool. My brother is two years younger than me. He's nine. But even though we are pretty close in age, it's still hard. We always get compared to each other. My parents think it's great that he's so good at baking, unlike me, and good at memorizing Quran. Again, not like me. So, just because they're bigger doesn't mean it's easier? We share a room and we have bunk beds, but he tries to jump off the top of them and gets in trouble! But sometimes it's fun when we talk before bedtime.

I've never had sisters but I wish I had one, or two! I think three sisters might be too many, though. ☺

Amena

P.S. Write back!!!

Dear Amena,

That's great that you can have a conversation with your brother ☺

Right now, with my sisters, not as much. My sisters sleep in cribs, but they still love jumping on my bed! My baby cousins do too. You're the only cousin (even though you're a second cousin) who's actually my age! Finally!

Nani and her brother (your grandfather) seem really close. I think they're lucky. Nani told me she's ten years older than her brother! So that makes me feel better whenever I imagine my sisters being older. Maybe then we'll be able to have real conversations?

I can't wait to see you next week at the aqiqah.

Rahma

Dear Rahma,

Not sure if this will get there in time before the aqiqah, but I'm excited to see you soon, your sisters, and alllll of our baby cousins.

I think babies are mostly cute. I think it'll be fun to meet.

We start our road trip tomorrow, so if I don't write back, it's because I'm not home! My brother and I always argue over what snacks to bring. We're allowed to buy one thing from the gas station. I want Sour Patch gummies but he wants Airheads, maybe because he is one. 😉

I hope I get Sour Patch gummies. The watermelon flavor is the best.

Amena

P.S. See you soon!

I stack Amena's postcards neatly into my palm. Nani was right. The postcards were more fun than I had thought.

Downstairs, I write "Sour Patch gummies (watermelon flavor)" on Mom's shopping list.

On the day of the aqiqah, I worry, what if Amena and I don't know what to say to each other? This could get awkward. What if we only get along through our postcards but have nothing to say in real life? I lie on my bed wondering if I even want to go to the aqiqah.

Hawwa walks in, knocking my new clothes on the floor before jumping on them, like a pile of leaves.

"Hawwa, you're ruining my clothes that Mom just ironed!"

Hawwa laughs each time she jumps onto my clothes. I try to grab them.

"Mooooom!" I yell.

"Get dressed!" yells Mom.

I ignore Hawwa.

"I'm trying!" I change into the new, now wrinkly clothes Nani has given me. This is my favorite outfit so far. It's a light blue shalwar kameez. I wonder if Amena will wear purple, her favorite color.

Even though we didn't look alike in Nani's baby photo, I wonder if she looks like me now that we're older.

"If you're ready, I need your help!" Mom calls from her room.

Baba and Mom's bedroom is a mess.

Khadeejah's sticking bows all over her hair and doesn't have any clothes on. Hawwa is halfway dressed and is now trying to grab Khadeejah's hair bows. Baba seems to be ignoring everyone somehow and is trimming his beard. Mom has on a silky kurta, but plaid pajamas on the bottom.

I sigh.

Mom does, too.

"Come on, Khadeejah!" I try to slip her kurta over her head. Khadeejah giggles as she runs away. Her belly jiggles.

"At least she's cute!" Baba smiles, trying to tickle her.

"I guess." I love how Khadeejah's cheeks puff out, but right now she's making us late. What if Amena's waiting for us? We need to hurry. I frantically grab Khadeejah while Baba puts the kurta over her head. Then the little shalwar. Finally little bangles that clink together when she runs. We're ready!

"Pwetty!" says Khadeejah as she looks in the mirror.

"Remember, Khadeejah, you're not just pretty. You're *smart*!" I respond.

Khadeejah giggles. "Pwetty and smart!"

On the way to the community center, I check my bag, making sure the Sour Patch watermelon gummies are in there. We've been part of the Maple Grove Community Center since I was a baby. My aqiqah took place here, too. Memories wash over me as Baba drives down the familiar roads.

The hall at the community center was also where my family held Khadeejah's and Hawwa's aqiqahs. I got a ton of gifts, and aunties congratulated me on being a big sister. I sat high up on Baba's shoulders when we cut the cake. I also got to eat the leftover slices and didn't have to share with anyone, unlike now. Plus, no one congratulates me or tells me I'm doing a good job as a big sister anymore, even though I got Khadeejah dressed today.

Inside the hall, colorful streamers decorate the ceiling. A balloon display dangles by a cake table. My eyes linger over the blue frosted cupcakes.

I visualize Khadeejah dipping her fingers into my cake frosting. I scan the hall for her. *Where's Khadeejah?*

I exhale when I see her riding on Baba's shoulders. Baba smiles down at me.

"Remember when you did this?"

My braid swishes as I nod.

"I can still give you a ride," offers Baba.

"No, Baba!" I shake my head. What if Amena walks in at that moment? That would be embarrassing!

But first, where *is* Amena? I scan the room and then run up to Nani, who is swaying with my baby cousin Waris. Waris looks fancy in his tiny blue sherwani. Nani does, too. She's wearing a turquoise abaya and silky hijab that shimmers like the sea.

"Nani!" I wave.

Nani doesn't hear me because there's a small circle of aunties who keep gathering around her and cooing over Waris. I guess it's not just Nani who loves aqiqahs and babies.

Typical.

"Nani!" I yell.

I had meant to tell her she looks nice, but instead, when Nani looks at me, I ask, "Where's Amena? I don't even know what she looks like now! All I saw was a baby picture!"

Nani nods. She hands Waris to Ghazala Khala

and looks around the room. There's another girl who looks my size, but I don't know if she's Amena or not. She could just be a girl who lives here in the Maple Grove community.

"Is that her?" I ask. I take a deep breath.

"They're not here yet, but they're on their way!" says Nani, checking her phone. As I wait, each minute feels longer and longer.

"There they are!" Nani points.

I turn expectantly. There she is, walking in with who I guess are her younger brother and grandfather. But wait a second. Are we wearing the *same* clothes? As she walks closer, our eyes narrow at each other at the same time.

My cousin is wearing the *exact* same outfit as me. It's like I'm looking in a mirror except... she's a foot taller than me. Otherwise, it could be like the movie *The Parent Trap*, where these two girls discover they're identical twins at summer camp. We even have our hair braided to the left.

I look up. She looks down. Then, as if on cue, each of us turns to look at Nani questioningly. The matching outfits are too much. I frown. Amena looks surprised and starts to frown back at me. I want to explain that I'm frowning because of the clothes, not because of her.

Both of us open our mouths to say something, but then a strong hand grabs our cheeks and turns our faces to Nani.

An overly enthusiastic, overly perfumed auntie holds us close.

"Zarina! What beauties. Sisters? You must have dressed them."

Nani bursts into chuckles. Little laughs escape Nani's mouth like little exhales of air.

"Cousins. I got both of their outfits at the Khaadi Eid sale! Two for the price of one! Available in all sizes!"

The auntie nods. "I can't resist a good sale, either!" The auntie kisses each of our cheeks before finally releasing our faces and wobbling away on her high heels.

"Yuck!" we both say at the same moment as we wipe frosty pink lipstick off our cheeks.

We look at each other and giggle at the same moment, too.

Phew. We're off to a better start now, thanks to Overly Perfumed Auntie.

Nani's brother's eyes crinkle as he pats me on the head. He also is a foot taller than Nani.

"You can call me Wahab Mamu. I see you met Amena. This is Hamzah."

Hamzah looks me in the eyes. "Why are you both wearing the same clothes? You don't look like twins. You're too short."

"Uh... My nani got them on sale," I answer.

"Boring!" He runs off.

Amena rolls her eyes. We both get quiet. I search my mind for something to talk about, but nothing comes up. We look away from each other. Maybe we're only good on paper.

Just then Khadeejah and Hawwa toddle over.

Amena bends way down to see them.

"You're so pretty!" She pats Khadeejah's pony-tails and then bends even lower to pat Hawwa's ponytails.

"I'm not pwetty. I'm *smart*!" sings Khadeejah.

Amena gives her two high fives. "Your sister *is* really smart! Who taught her to say that? She's only two years old!"

"I taught her that today," I answer, glad for the distraction.

"Come, let's greet the guests," says Nani to Amena and me, putting her arms around our shoulders.

As Nani kisses an older lady, I say salaam to my friend Halima, who's wearing a sparkly orange shalwar kameez.

"This is Halima. And this is my cousin Amena." I say, introducing them.

"Nice to meet you, Amena," Halima says. "My cousin is here, too," she adds, pointing to a boy with curly hair named Rehan. Rehan and Hamzah look like they're stocking up on goody bags until Halima's grandmother pushes Rehan in front of Nani and says, "You must hear him recite Quran, it's so beautiful."

We greet a few more guests until we're allowed

to wander off on our own. I'm eager to sit and talk to Amena alone, but Khadeejah keeps running up to me and tickling me. I flush with anger.

"Khadeejah, GO AWAY! Go to Mom, okay?"

Khadeejah's face crumples as she walks away.

I brush away a flicker of guilt and quickly ask Amena how she makes such great crayon roses.

"I can show you exactly how I make the roses," volunteers Amena as she pulls out crayons and paper from her bag.

"That would be great!"

My shoulders relax when I realize it's easy to talk to her. I don't feel that shy dry mouth feeling around her and it feels like I've known her longer than a few minutes.

Suddenly, Mom rushes up to me, interrupting. "Have you seen Khadeejah?"

"She was just here. I told her to go away to you. . . ." I swallow and look around the room but only see Hawwa with Baba. My head droops when I think of telling Khadeejah to go away. I just wanted some alone time with my cousin.

Mom's face is tight with worry. Amena takes one look at her and says, "We'll help you look." She calls Hamzah over to join the search. My heart beats loudly as I scan the room. My little sister can't just disappear, can she? Where did she go? I didn't really mean for her to go away! Tears poke my eyes when after a few minutes we still haven't found her. Everyone has stopped talking and is searching for her now.

Just as a sob is about to escape my lips, Hamzah shouts, "FOUND HER!"

Khadeejah claps her hands as she peers from under the tablecloth on the goody bag table. Her hands are all sticky from M&M's.

"Khadeejah!" I hug my little sister tight. My heart beats slower. Mom and Baba join the hug before Mom picks up Khadeejah and leads her away.

"Even though my little sisters are a handful, I can't imagine life without them..." I whisper. Amena runs up to me. Her face is serious, and she nods like she totally understands.

"You're a good big sister."

I stand taller. I fish out the bag of Sour Patch watermelon gummies from my bag and hand it to Amena.

"Hey, you got me my favorite gummies! Wow! Writing postcards was a great idea! Thank you!" Amena smiles. I notice that we each have a dimple in our left cheek.

I'm just about to tell her when a hand swoops between us, grabs the gummies, and disappears.

"Who was that?" I look at Amena.

Amena shakes her head in dismay. "I'm going to get him!"

Before I understand what's happening, Amena's thrown off her silver party shoes and is chasing Hamzah underneath and around the balloon arc. Hamzah is shorter but fast. He cackles and holds the gummies high as he runs.

I join Amena and zoom after him. Khadeejah runs after me. Hawwa toddles after her. A minute later, Amena pins him down. I grab the gummies. Out of breath, we rip open the bag.

“You could have just asked for a gummy instead of stealing them!” scolds Amena.

Hamzah pants.

“Fine, may I pleeeeeeeeeeeease have a gummy?” he asks, holding out his palm.

Amena drops one in his palm.

“Just one?” he whines.

“Yup.”

I giggle.

“Here.” She pours a handful in my palm.

“No fair!” groans Hamzah.

“No fair!” echoes Khadeejah.

The sweet and sour gummies make my lips purse as I chew. Khadeejah puts her head on my lap and looks up at Amena expectantly.

“Here you go!” Amena gives Khadeejah a couple of gummies. “Your sisters are adorable!” she gushes to me.

Hamzah gently helps Hawwa up from the floor after she’s tripped on her dupatta.

“Your brother’s not so bad, either!” pops out of

my mouth, and I cover it in surprise. But it's true, I realize. He found Khadeejah.

Amena watches Hamzah help Hawwa and rewards him by giving him more gummies.

"Time for family photos!" yells Nani, holding up her camera. Her arms jingle with the gold bangles that she wore especially for today's event.

"That means us!" I grab Amena's hand and walk toward Nani.

"Hey, I still have some postcards..." whispers Amena as we stand next to each other for the family photo.

"Me too..." I whisper back.

"Want to stay pen pals?"

"Of course! We can email, too." I glance at Nani, who commands, "Enough talking! More smiling! Like this!"

Nani shows all her teeth in an exaggerated smile.

"Totally." Amena giggles. "Or FaceTime?"

I glance around the hall, which is full of happiness, memories, and people I love, and grin extra wide, just like Nani told us to.

Dear Amena,

I had so much fun meeting you! I'm so glad we're related and can't wait to see you again! Hopefully LOTS of times!

I'm glad you thought Hawwa and Khadeejah were adorable. I sometimes complain about them . . . okay, maybe I complain about them a lot! 😉, but I agree with you. They're adorable-ish.

You know how Sour Patch gummies are sweet and sour? I think that's what having a brother or sister is all about. Sometimes there are some sour moments, but you just have to look for the sweetness. It's right here.

Love,

Rahma

P.S. Nani says we'll get to visit you for Thanksgiving!

P.P.S. Write back!

A TASTE OF SOMETHING NEW

by Simran Jeet Singh

"I HATE INDIAN FOOD," I MUMBLE AS I STARE AT MY plate. There's a green blob of palak paneer staring right back at me. It feels like I've eaten the same food and smelled the same smells every day of my life. Couldn't we just have pasta for once?

"You're so dramatic about food," Neena says, rolling her eyes at me from across the dinner table. "And picky."

"I'm not!" I argue. "I eat everything they serve in the school cafeteria. Enchiladas. Pizza. Turkey sandwiches. Even those mashed potatoes that stick to the tray, no matter how hard you bang it against the trash can."

"Nasty!" Neena wrinkles her nose. "If you can eat all that stuff and hate Indian food, then you're a self-racist."

"Taste buds aren't racist," I shoot back. "You're allergic to milk. Does that make you racist against cows?"

"That makes no sense," Neena scoffs. She rolls her eyes again, this time at my parents.

I know that already, of course. But as her little brother, I have two jobs: to disagree with anything she says and to get under her skin.

"Sure, it makes sense," I insist. "Cows can be black, brown, or white. So, what do you have against them?"

"That doesn't make any sense, either," Neena quips, clearly annoyed.

She's right again. But I'm smiling now. *Mission accomplished.*

What really doesn't make sense, even to me, is why I don't like Indian food. Well, I like some of it—the breads, the rice, the yogurt. And especially the dessert. Even beans and lentils are fine. But I'm so tired of any dish made with vegetables, which in Punjabi we refer to as sabji. They all taste the same to me now, no matter what's in them—potatoes, peas, eggplant, okra. My parents say that I used to eat it all as a baby, no problem. But for as long as *I* can remember, I've struggled to eat it. I've tried all kinds of tricks, like dousing my sabji in dahi and pinching my nose when I eat. Thank God for the breads and rice and yogurt. They're the only things that keep my stomach half-full during an Indian meal.

Maybe taste buds aren't racist, but when it comes to sabji, mine are definitely discriminating.

My distaste for Indian food comes up in conversation all the time, which I hate too, by the way. Any time we're with other people, whether they're South Asian or not, someone brings it up, as if it's a fascinating piece of trivia.

Hai! Jeevan, you don't like Indian food? But aren't you Indian?

You might think, like I did, that no one would care about what someone else eats or doesn't eat. It's not like I go around judging people for their food preferences. But for some reason, people do care, and even worse, they're so dramatic about it, like it's the biggest deal in the world.

YOU DON'T LIKE INDIAN FOOD? OH MY GOSH! I THINK I'M HAVING A HEART ATTACK!

It doesn't matter if they're close family members or strangers on an airplane. I know what they're going to say because they all say the exact same thing: *How could you not like Indian food? It's so good.*

Then they'll share their opinions, or their

anecdotes, or their theories, as if I care about any of that.

One thing I do care about is not making my parents feel bad. But they know that about me and use it to their advantage. Like many South Asian parents, they love a good guilt trip.

We're sitting on the couches in the living room, watching the Nets game after dinner, and as she does often, Mom offers a random comment to no one in particular: "Do you know how much Americans pay for desi khana? Twenty dollars a plate! We're so lucky to have this food at home for free."

Dad guffaws, as if she said something unbelievable, as if LeBron James had just been elected president of the entire universe and was going to make candy the new currency.

"Twenty dollars a plate? Everyone loves our food so much. We really shouldn't be taking it for granted."

I roll my eyes at his fake surprise. I know that by "we," he means "me," but I also know better than to be baited into an argument. We literally have this same conversation once a week, and I've learned that disagreeing only makes them double down and that ignoring them makes them angry.

Instead, I offer a half smile and nod my head in agreement, as if they're making good points that I'm planning to accept. As if my taste buds will suddenly change their minds and start liking sabji again.

Usually I keep nodding and smiling until they get bored and move on, but this time feels different. Instead of talking about how scarce food was during his childhood like he usually does, Dad pulls at his watchband and takes a deep breath, the telltale sign that he is about to make an announcement.

I look over at him. He looks at Neena, who looks at my mom, who looks at me. Everyone knows the news except for me, which can only mean trouble.

"Jeevan," he says. "I wanted to tell you something exciting."

Okay...

"I signed you up for a new class."

Okay...

"It's not the kind of classes you've done before...."

Hmmmm.

"I think it's good for you to branch out and try new things besides sports."

Uh-oh.

"And also, no other kids signed up and I was feeling bad for Prem Auntie."

Wait, what?

"The thing is, your mother and I think it will be good for you to spend some time with her and develop an appreciation for our cultural cuisine."

Oh no!

"So, we enrolled you in her new Indian cooking class at the community center."

Seriously? How could they sign me up for something without asking me? I'm old enough to make my own decisions.

"Unfortunately, it's at the same time as the pickup basketball games at the center. So, you'll have to miss those."

I realize that everyone is watching me, waiting to see how I'll react. Usually I'm pretty open about sharing how I feel. But now, I feel so hurt and angry that I don't even know what to say. So, I sit there silently.

My mom knows me better than anyone, and after a minute, she breaks the silence.

"Beta, I understand you're upset and that it's not fair to sign you up without asking you," she says. "The thing is, since Prem Auntie's husband passed away, she's feeling lonely at home. She helped us so much when we first moved to this country, and we want to help her now."

I knew that Inderjit Uncle had died recently, but I hadn't thought about how Auntie must be feeling. To be honest, I never really think about Auntie at all. She's been in our lives for as long as I can remember, but always in the background. She was always at the community center events whenever we went there, yet through all the years, I don't think we ever said more than ten sentences to each other.

I try to see it from my mom's side. She's just trying to help a friend who needs it.

"I get it, Mom," I say, trying to be mature. "But why can't Neena take the class instead of me? She's older, and she actually likes Indian food."

"We thought about that," Mom says. "But Neena has her math tutoring on Saturday afternoons. This was the only option we had, and we really wouldn't have done it if we had any other choice."

I stare at the TV, and it stares back at me. And a few moments into our staring contest, I decide to offer a compromise. "Mom. If she's feeling lonely, what if I offer to just hang out with her for an hour a week? I mean, I don't want to do that either, honestly—but you know how much I hate sabji. And then I won't have to miss basketball games, either."

My mom glances at my dad, a clear sign that this isn't going to work. "I offered to spend time with her already, beta. In fact, I gave her a number of different suggestions. But Prem Auntie insisted that she pass on a 'life skill' to the next generation, and that this be it."

"Thanks for trying," I sigh, realizing that I'm stuck.

"Thank you," she says, and leans over to kiss me. I can tell she means it. I also know deep down that she hopes this class will cure my weirdness about eating sabji.

I return to my staring contest. My stomach somersaults. Tomorrow's going to suck.

Saturdays are usually my favorite. Dad makes waffles with berries for breakfast. Then he takes me to my rock climbing class while Mom takes Neena for tae kwon do before her afternoon tutoring.

This Saturday morning is dreary, though. It's cold and rainy, and I wake up with a pit in my stomach.

Before I even get out of bed, Neena comes in to deliver more bad news. "Hey, twerp, Coach Courtney just called. Your climbing session this morning is canceled."

I groan and throw my pillow at the window in frustration.

"Hey, are you okay? It's just a class, right?"

I don't usually like to tell Neena how I'm feeling because I know it gives her more ammo to pick on me. But I'm so upset that I don't care right now. "I literally just woke up and today is already the worst," I tell her. "Now that I can't play basketball, rock climbing was going to be the only fun thing this weekend. And now all I have is this cooking class because some auntie feels lonely."

"I'm sorry, Jeevan," she responds, with a softness I don't hear in her voice often. "I tried to tell them not to sign you up, and I even tried to change my tutoring schedule so I could take the class so that you wouldn't have to. I know how much this sucks for you."

"Thanks," I mumble, and then wait for her to leave.

Once she's gone, I decide to try one more thing. I roll out of bed and stumble into my parents' room, holding my belly.

"Mom, Dad," I whisper hoarsely. "I'm not feeling well at all."

Dad looks at me with concern, but Mom isn't falling for it.

"Oh sorry, beta. Good thing your class was canceled. Let's get you some rest so that you have energy for Prem Auntie's class this afternoon."

I walk out of their room and go back to mine.

I spend the rest of the morning sulking.

"Why aren't you eating your breakfast?" Dad asks.

"I'm not hungry."

"Do you want the sports section of the paper?" Mom asks.

"Nah."

"Do you want to play video games before I go for tae kwon do class?" Neena asks.

"Thanks, but no thanks."

I figure that if I do nothing, then at least the worst day ever can't get any worse.

At two p.m., Dad comes to my room to get me.

"Ready?" he asks, hopeful for a response.

I don't say anything and shuffle my feet to the car.

"You doing okay, bud?" he asks as we buckle our seat belts.

I shrug my shoulders and stare out the window, as if there's anything interesting to see in Maple Grove.

We spend the half-hour drive to the community center in silence. When we pull up in the parking lot, I can see the day actually *could* get worse—and that it just did.

All of my friends are on the basketball court. Literally, *all* of them. Dad notices, too.

I get out of the car and begin walking toward the front door. Before I get there, my dad puts his arm around my shoulders and makes an offer.

"Hey, J-Man, I know you're upset and I understand. How about this? You get through today's class, and if you hate it, I'll talk to your mother about canceling the rest. Just remember what Michael Jordan always said."

"Live the moment for the moment," we both say together.

I can tell he's trying to compromise, and while I'm still annoyed to be there, the tension in my body softens slightly.

"Thanks, Dad. That sounds fine."

Then we walk together, through the front doors of the community center and toward the kitchen in the back.

I don't see any other kids in the kitchen, just uncles and aunties singing "Vahiguru" as they dump beans and rice and spices into pots big enough to hold me. The sabji smell is so overpowering that I think for a moment about jumping in one of the empty pots and closing the lid over myself. But then it occurs to me that someone might accidentally put that pot on the stove without realizing I was in there, or even worse, pour the sizzling thadka right on top of me.

I spot Prem Auntie standing at the counter near the center. She is a tiny human, and she looks even smaller in the massive kitchen, especially with all these other people bustling about behind her. In addition to being tiny, Auntie is also older than time. Her face is small and puckered, like she's trying desperately to hold in her dentures. And if you look closely at her hands, you'll notice that even her wrinkles have wrinkles.

Of course, I would never say that to anyone because we're supposed to respect our elders. So instead, as we walk into the massive kitchen and I see her tiny frame inside of it, I fold my hands and lower my gaze and greet her with a gentle sassrikal. Dad reaches down to touch her feet, and I follow his lead. I try not to cringe when she places her haldi-stained hands on my head to bless me. I know old age isn't contagious—but it still kind of freaks me out.

She then pulls me in for a hug so tight and long that I can barely breathe for ten seconds. If I'm being honest, that hug is a godsend, not because I like overly affectionate auntie hugs but because not being able to breathe also means ten seconds of not having to smell the fresh sabji cooking in the kitchen.

When she lets go, she squeals, in a pitch you'd think only dogs could hear:

"So happy to have you here, young man! It's so nice to know you love the delicious food of our culture so much."

Not quite.

"You are going to be amazing at cooking all the Punjabi dishes that you love—daal, cholay, saag paneer, karaylay."

My stomach turns.

"You're the only person who signed up for this class, which means lucky you will have one-on-one mentoring from your auntie for the next two months."

Just like this morning, it does a full somersault.

She turns to Dad. "Thank you again for supporting this class. You can pick Jeevan up in two hours."

It nearly plummets.

She reaches up to squeeze my cheeks. "Your wife is going to be so lucky to have found you."

"Excuse me," I say, and hurry to the stairwell.

I sit on the steps, needing a moment to process everything. But of course, this being the worst day ever, Vikram and Nikhil happen to come down the stairs just then.

"Hey, J," Nikhil exclaims with his trademark enthusiasm. "Basketball's going to be awesome today, right?"

"Definitely." I squeeze out a smile. I don't want them to know what I'm really up to. "Let me just do a couple of things with my dad and then I'll come out."

They fill up their water bottles and head back out, which is my cue to return to my class.

I'm not quite sure what to say to Prem Auntie about why I stepped away, but thankfully, she doesn't ask. Maybe she and Dad discussed my disdain for sabji while I was in the stairwell, or maybe not. Either way, we all pretend like nothing has happened.

"I'll be back in an hour or two," announces my dad. He winks at me, as if to say, *Just get through today's class and you won't have to come back.*

"Sounds good," I say, but I don't wink back at him. I may not be as mad as I was before, but that doesn't mean I'm happy to be here.

Oblivious to my annoyance, Auntie hands me a massive bag of tomatoes to wash. While I do that, she pulls out two sharp knives and two cutting boards. Then we stand shoulder to shoulder and start chopping.

Next, we move on to peeling and chopping onions. My eyes sting from the onion vapors, and one of the other aunties brings us goggles. I recognize her as Ajay's mom and offer her a sassrikal and a side hug. I usually see her and Mohan Uncle and Ajay at the community center on Sundays for religious classes and services. There are some other gurdwaras around, but my parents and some of their friends say those are too big and that they prefer to be in a smaller, more tight-knit community. So, they rent the community center instead.

I actually really like coming here every Sunday, and I'd like it even more if they had left the langar tradition behind. While I like the idea of langar—that everyone sits on the floor and has a meal together after learning and praying together—there's usually a sabji or two served with it. And you know how I feel about that. People judge if you skip the sabji. Trust me, I've tried. To avoid judgment and to avoid having to eat it, I usually spend the entire mealtime serving food to others.

"You should eat too, beta," the aunties say.

"Shaabash," the uncles praise me. "So much seva. Such a good boy."

I'm glad they don't know the real reason I serve food rather than sitting down to eat it.

I notice that the kitchen is busy today too as aunties and uncles busily prepare langar. It's strange because today's Saturday and the community center is pretty empty.

I ask Prem Auntie as the questions come to me: "Who are all these people? And who are they cooking all this food for?"

"Every Saturday, a handful of the Sikhs from around New Jersey cook and deliver langar to people around the community who don't have access to food," she explains.

I know about poverty and hunger, of course, and I even know that the Sikh tradition of langar is open to people of all backgrounds. But I have only ever seen people coming to the gurdwara to eat langar, both in America and in Punjab. I have never heard of taking langar to the people who needed it.

"That's such an amazing idea," I respond, realizing this could also get me out of the cooking class. "Could I maybe join for the delivery?"

"Of course you can, beta. But before you learn to share, you must learn to prepare."

I'm not sure what she means by that, but it sounds cryptic and wise, like something Yoda would say. So, I shrug my shoulders, say "Acha," and go on chopping onions.

Prem Auntie then passes me a stack of ginger and a peeler, which grosses me out, because as rough as ginger looks, it tastes even rougher. Even its Punjabi word is rough on one's mouth: "adhrak"? More like adh-yuck.

I'm surprised to realize that even though I don't like ginger, I do enjoy peeling it. I find myself getting into a rhythm. As the volunteers say "Vahi," I reach forward and touch the peeler to the adhrak. As they exhale "Guru," I exhale too, pulling the peeler back toward me.

My body relaxes, which surprises me as well, because I didn't even know it was tense in the first place.

"I'm impressed that you're here. I used to hate cooking when I was your age." Auntie turns to me while mincing her garlic.

It's easy to imagine Prem Auntie as a kid. She'd be about the same height and have the same high-pitched voice. But it's hard to imagine her hating cooking. I don't know her that well, but she's a Punjabi auntie, and don't those two things go hand in hand?

"Why?" I ask.

"Well, same as you, probably. It takes a lot of patience, and I would have rather been having fun with my friends. But when my mother died, my father had to work late hours to help support our family. My brothers and I had no choice but to take care of one another. We all learned to cook, but it wasn't until much later that I started to enjoy it."

Maybe Auntie understands me more than I think.

"Do you enjoy it now, or do you cook because you have to?"

"Good question, Jeevan. I do enjoy it now. Those other things are still true. It still takes patience, and I'd prefer to relax with the people I love. But I've learned a lot from cooking, and it's made me a better person. I now think of cooking as a spiritual practice."

I've never heard of cooking as a spiritual practice, and I can't imagine that rolling rotis can make you a better person. But I figure it's best to let her keep talking.

"When you cook, you have to be in the moment. You can't be focused on the past and what you could have done or should have done. And you can't even really focus on the future and how you hope things will be. You just have to focus on the present, and make sure you're doing everything correctly, step-by-step, minute by minute."

Prem Auntie hands me a bucket filled with okra, or as Mom calls them, lady fingers. After Auntie tells me what to do, I wash them in the sink and bring them back to the cutting board. I square up each piece so I can slice off the top and the bottom without cutting my hand. Then I cut each "finger" into four pieces, carefully placing my knife near the tip of my own finger.

I do about ten of them before pausing to look up and say, "I see what you mean." I turn back to the okra on my cutting board, my mind emptied of all its distractions. No basketball game, no friends outside, no waffles with berries. Not even any sabji smells that had been overpowering me just minutes before. It's just me and the okra, one-on-one.

Prem Auntie and I work in silence for the next five minutes, neither of us saying anything. The only sound behind us is the gentle repetition of "Vahiguru" from the aunties and uncles in the background.

I remember the quote from Michael Jordan that Dad reminded me of earlier: "Live the moment for the moment."

If Jordan told us *what* we should do, maybe Prem Auntie had figured out *how* to do it, at least to some degree. For her, cooking was a way to live in the moment. Maybe the same could be true for me, too.

"So, is that when you started to enjoy cooking?" I ask, while sliding the okra tips from the cutting board into the garbage.

"Ki cheez, beta?"

I pour the rest of the okra into a bowl before clarifying. "I mean, is that what changed for you? You stopped seeing cooking as something you *had* to do and started seeing it as a spiritual practice and a way to serve people?"

"I guess so, beta." She fires up the stove and grabs a pan bigger than my face. Then she continues. "I'm really going to miss it if they close this place down."

"What do you mean, close it down? Are they talking about that?"

This time Prem Auntie wrinkles her nose, as if there's an unpleasant scent *she* wants to avoid. "Pass me the tayl, beta."

She pours in a ton of oil. Without looking at me, she adds, "I guess if you haven't heard about it, it's a good thing. Don't worry."

I'm intrigued, but just as I'm about to ask her for more information, she throws the thadka and the diced onions into the pan. The sizzle begins almost immediately, and I brace myself for a visceral reaction. But to my surprise, the familiar aroma of cumin seeds and diced onions doesn't bother me.

Prem Auntie lifts the cutting board. I slide the chopped okra into the pan. The sizzle intensifies briefly. And as the sounds settle, I notice that the bhindi, a type of sabji, almost smells sweet.

Don't get me wrong. Its greenish-yellow glow still looks radioactive to me. I'm not about to put that into my body, let alone my mouth.

But I didn't have to run out of the room. Am I making progress?

Prem Auntie squeezes my cheeks and says, "Beta, this week you learned about preparing. Next week, we'll focus on sharing."

She hands me a stack of empty containers, and I know just what to do with them. They're the same reused yogurt cartons that my mom uses for packing sabji at home.

We stand next to each other, pouring food into the containers as we listen to the steady stream of "Vahiguru. Vahiguru. Vahiguru." I feel my body relaxing again, and I feel kind of weightless, almost as if I'm floating in the ocean. I lose track of time.

Suddenly, a distant voice snaps me out of my trance.

"Hey, Jeevan, is that you? You coming to play?"

I look over my shoulder and see Alok and Rohit at the water cooler just outside the kitchen. I walk over to them and play it cool.

"Yeah, I'm around. I'm just tired. I'll come play in a bit."

"If you're tired, then make sure that I get to guard you." Alok's always talking trash.

“I could beat you in my sleep,” I reply. “But seriously, I’ll be out to play in a few minutes.”

I’m almost in the clear when Prem Auntie pokes her head out of the kitchen and blows my cover. “Jeevan, beta. Please finish packing the bhindi.”

“Hanji, Auntie,” I say quietly.

Alok and Rohit both give me a funny look.

“Wait, are you eating bhindi? I thought you hated that stuff,” whispers Alok.

“I do.”

“Dude, wait,” Rohit half whispers and half shouts. “Are you taking Prem Auntie’s cooking class?!”

“No way,” adds Alok, before I can say anything. “I would have never guessed that.”

Now they’re both bewildered. I guess I’m famous for hating sabji. But I can tell they’re not judging me. They’re more curious than anything.

“Yeah,” I say quietly, trying to not make a big deal out of it. “I’m just doing it for today because my parents felt bad for her. It’s not like I’m really taking her class.”

"Well, can you ditch it, then, and come play with us instead?" asks Rohit.

I think about it for a moment, and at first, I'm inclined to say yes. But then I think about how kind Prem Auntie has been to me and how disappointed she'd be if I didn't come back to the kitchen and finish what I started.

I turn to my friends and can't believe the words that come out of my mouth. "You guys go ahead and play. I have to finish up this class with Auntie. But I'll come out as soon as we're done."

Alok's eyebrows go up, and then his shoulders go up, too. I don't think he ever imagined me picking Indian food over basketball. To be honest, I didn't, either.

But here I am, cooking with Prem Auntie on a Saturday afternoon. I walk back over to her and continue pouring the greenish-yellow bhindi into small containers. I fall back into the rhythm. "Vahiguru. Vahiguru. Vahiguru." And after a while, I notice something else, too. I'm not holding my breath anymore.

It's not like I'm about to eat the food. But I'm not grossed out by it anymore. I'm grateful for that and am surprised to realize that even though I'm still not interested in eating the actual food, I'm already looking forward to returning next week to cook with Prem Auntie.

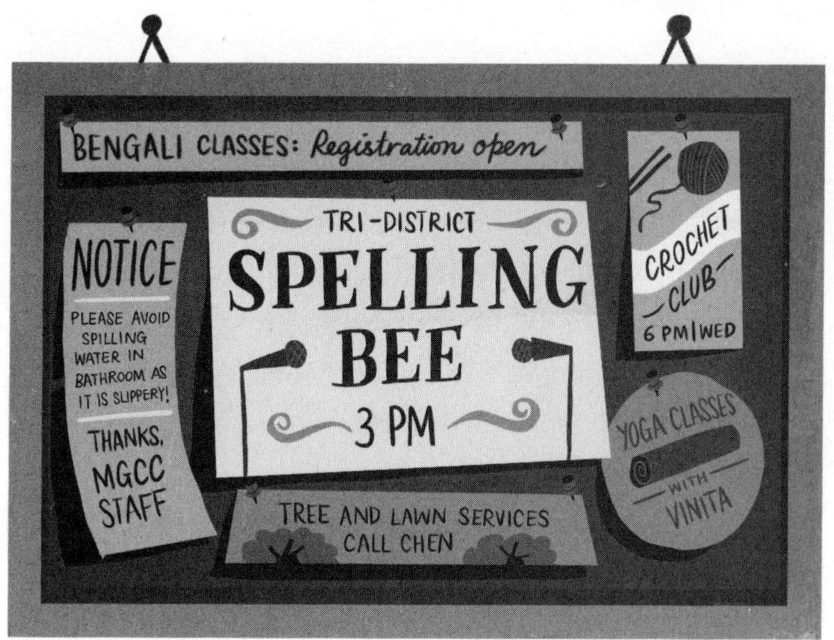

HOW TO SPELL "DISASTER"

by Supriya Kelkar

IF YOU'VE EVER WATCHED THE SCRIPPS NATIONAL Spelling Bee, you know it's a big deal. It's, like, the Super Bowl of spelling bees, the Oscars for spellers, the Olympics for words. You get the point. It's major. And the kids in it are basically celebrities.

They even have little videos in between the competition, showing the famous spellers memorizing tons of words in different kinds of dictionaries, their parents proudly beaming at them.

That's pretty much my life all the time. Except I'm not the kid the parents are proud of. Nope. That's my little sister, Nisha.

She started spelling at twenty-two months old. The local news even did a story on her when she was four, where a reporter and camerawoman followed us around for a whole day, filming Nisha as she practiced with her spelling coach in our kitchen and read a giant dictionary on the swing in our backyard. And now, at age six, she's pretty much a shoo-in for Scripps. And our entire life is about spelling.

I can't tell you how many spelling bees I've been to. I can't tell you how many times I've watched kids onstage ask judges for the language of origin for a word they have to spell. Or ask the judge to use it in a sentence.

Usually that kid is Nisha. She has so many

words memorized, so many languages of origin, so many practice sentences, I've lost count. She is the reigning under-15 spelling bee champ of our state this year, and the *Maple Grove Dispatch* has done tons of stories about her over the past few months.

I don't mind her getting all the attention. I'm proud of her, too. But I kind of wish part of my life got to be more about another eight-letter word that starts with "s" and ends with "ing": swimming. I'm practically like a fish in the water. Well, not a flying gurnard, which would rather walk on the seafloor than swim. But like other fish. The ones who love swimming. Because I love swimming. I love being in the water. I love helping other people in the water. It's my thing. This Friday evening, though, instead of getting to go to my Junior Lifeguard class on the far side of town, I have to go to something that will probably end up in a video at Scripps this summer, just a part of Nisha's backstory.

Why make waves when you can just go with the flow, I guess?

"I'm sorry you have to miss your class," Nisha says to me from her car seat, about to chew the end of one of her curls in a pre-bee jitters habit, before I cringe and shake my head to stop her.

"Oh, it doesn't matter, shona," Aai says to her from the driver's seat of our car, as she turns the wheel and we enter the community center parking lot. She glances at me. "You'll have fun playing basketball with the other kids, Sanjay."

I sigh, watching Aai's red, crescent-shaped tikli on her forehead in the rearview mirror.

"And don't worry about missing lifeguard class. You can make it up next week," Baba adds, fiddling with the radio until he finds the perfect volume for the Bollywood hits playing from it.

I gently rub my tongue over my braces, which can cut me like Baba's words. This is a disaster. *I'm never going to be certified if I miss every week*, I think to myself. Aai and Baba should know this. They should know how much it matters to me. They should know I don't care that it's all the way across town at the exact same time as this bee; I still want to be there. They should have known it is the one place where I am really good at something, better than Nisha. They should have known all of this without my having to *spell* it out for them.

Nisha looks at me, her eyes widening as Aai parks the car. "I'd feel bad if I had to miss spelling. Maybe next week we can all come and watch you save the manikins at camp, Sanjay dada," she adds, using the Marathi title for big brother. "That's M-A-N-I-K-I-N-S, for anyone wondering. If they were in a store and used to model clothes, it would be M-A-N-N-E-Q-U-I-N-S."

I turn to Nisha. She's about to go for her curls again, the thought of which makes me want to gag. "I'm really good at saving them. And you're really good at spelling them. So don't worry about me today. Just think about winning at the bee," I say, as she lets go of her hair. "I know you're going to do great. G-R-A-T-E." I grin, trying to ease her nerves.

Nisha groans. "Sanjay dada!"

"Sanjay! Don't confuse her," Baba lectures.

"She won't get confused over a short word like that," Aai replies confidently as we unbuckle and head out.

"I'm kidding," I say, moving my black waves out of my eyes and rushing into the community center with my family. I *was* joking, but clearly, I'm also a better junior lifeguard than a speller because if you asked me to use "grate" or "great" in a sentence, I'd probably freeze up, thinking about everyone listening to me, and I definitely don't know the language of origin for either of them.

The community center is bustling with kids and parents running to different rooms. I pause at the bulletin board. There is Hindi/Urdu class today; math class; bharatanatyam and kathak dance classes; a bunch of different yoga classes; a seniors meet-up, where a bunch of grandparents get together to socialize; and, of course, today's main event: the spelling bee.

"Okay, we'll be in the hall," Aai says, scanning the board. "Will you be outside with your friends, Sanjay?"

I nod. Although I'm not sure how many actual friends will be there. I'm not in the mood to have to find a way to make friends with a bunch of strangers, like a fish being forced to join a school he knows no one in.

Priyanka Auntie, a tall woman with long, shiny black hair, waves to us from down the hall. "Hi, Nisha! Ready to do your best?"

Nisha points to the spaceship on her shirt. "Ready to be out of this universe. U-N-I-V-E-R-S-E."

Priyanka Auntie grins. "Perfect! We're about to start," she adds as she nears us. "And hi, Sanjay beta. Still so scrawny! Look at those arms."

I flinch, knowing what is coming next. As if on cue, Priyanka Auntie ruffles my hair, making it go in every direction.

Ugh. I hate when she does that. And she *always* does that. It has been her standard greeting for me since I was a toddler with a huge mop of curls softened with ayurvedic sesame seed oil on my head. Why doesn't she get that I am eleven now and it's embarrassing to have your head patted like a dog when you didn't ask for it? And what makes her think it's nice to talk about what I look like? I am super flexible and double-jointed. It means my elbows turn a little differently than hers and I don't have a lot of muscle on my arms. My parents explained that to her years ago, but she still always makes a comment about my arms.

"I'm going to stop by the bee in a little bit," I say, trying to flatten my hair back into place. "Good luck, Nisha," I add, bending down to hug my little sister.

"Thanks," she says, beaming.

"See you in a bit," Baba says, squeezing my hand bye before he, Aai, Nisha, and Priyanka Auntie race down the hall as fast as a mako shark, which just happens to be one of the fastest fish in the ocean.

I head for the back doors to the community center. The glass is smudged with a hundred little handprints from all the kids who go through here for different classes. Through the blurry door, I can make out a handful of kids on the basketball court at the end of the parking lot. I take a deep breath, like I do before I jump off a diving board, and push the door open.

"You're not watching the bee?" a voice asks behind me.

I turn. It's Halima. Her younger brother has been doing the spelling bee as long as Nisha has.

I shrug. "I thought I'd go there in a bit."

She nods, her voice dropping to a whisper. "It *is* kind of boring."

I let out a small laugh. "Are Nora and Sandeep doing the bee today?"

"Yup. Same group as always. Don't worry, us bad spellers won't be missed."

We near the group of kids playing basketball by the fence separating the community center parking lot from the neighborhood. There are Sakura and Ren, the tall twins who play on our school's basketball teams, and Andrea, a girl I took swimming classes with at the local pool when we were younger. Akshay, a boy whose dad knows my dad from when they were in high school in India, dribbles quickly around me and Halima. And a kid I haven't seen before, who is holding a bag of gummy worms in one hand while dribbling his neon pink basketball with the other, eyes me up and down.

Halima and I say hi to everyone, but instead of saying hi back, the boy with the gummy worms shouts, "Think fast!"

Before I can even *think* about what I'm supposed to think fast about, a pink blur comes flying toward me.

I throw my hands out a few seconds too late, and the basketball hits me right between the ribs.

"Ow," I groan, rubbing the spot.

"Why would you do that?" Halima scowls, throwing the ball back at the boy.

"It was just a joke," the boy says, nearing me to shove the wrinkled plastic bag of colorful, fruit-flavored worms near my face.

"Want some?" he asks.

I frown, moving my face back, my chest still hurting, kind of like my feelings. First the ball, now this. Doesn't this kid know what personal space means, or do I have to spell that out for him? "No thanks," I say, shoving down my irritated thoughts.

"Don't worry. I have braces, too. They don't get stuck in them that much," the boy says.

I shake my head, breathing a little easier as the pain subsides. "I'm vegetarian," I reply. "Gummy worms usually have gelatin in them."

"Well then," the boy says, widening his eyes, pretending to be offended while Ren giggles and Sakura nudges her brother to stop.

Halima rolls her eyes. "I'm Halima. What's your name?"

"Vikram," the boy replies, grinning widely.

I swallow down the hot flash of nausea that is trying to creep up my throat at the sight of bits and pieces of purple and green gummy worms jammed in his braces.

"Gross," Halima says, cringing a little as Vikram laughs loudly, clearly enjoying the attention.

"What?" Vikram grins. "I said they don't get

stuck *that* much. Just *this* much," he adds pointing to his teeth.

This kid is like my polar opposite. Someone who loves to be the center of attention. It's like he is a baleen whale, whose voice can travel farther than any other animal's voice in the world. And I am a timid little Great Barrier Reef blenny, trying to swim through this world without being heard.

"This is my friend Sanjay," Halima says, changing the subject away from the gummy worms. "His sister and my brother are in the spelling bee right now."

"Chest pass!" Vikram abruptly throws his ball at my torso hard, and I just manage to block it.

Again? He threw it at me again with barely any warning. It's like he'll do anything to have the spotlight on him, no matter who gets a ball chucked in their face in the process.

"Vikram!" Akshay frowns as he picks up the ball and rebounds it.

"What?" Vikram shrugs innocently. "I just wanted him to play with us."

"You could have hurt him," Andrea says, talking about me like I'm not even there. But I guess that's okay, since I don't really feel like talking about my feelings the way Nisha is probably talking about words inside the hall.

"Hurt. *May I have the definition?"*

"To cause pain or injury to."

"Would you use it in a sentence, please?"

"It hurts *when Priyanka Auntie makes fun of my arms and rubs my head without my consent. It* hurts *when Vikram throws a basketball at my chest without any warning, twice; my chest and palms still sting from the impact. And it really, really* hurts *when Aai and Baba make me miss lifeguard class for a local spelling bee that I'm not even in because they don't realize how much I like this class or that I go to every local spelling bee my sister is in, so 'what's the big deal if I miss one?'"*

Whoops. I guess I used "hurt" in way more than just one sentence.

"Yeah," Halima adds. "And if you ever get hurt out here, he's the only one who could help. He's a junior lifeguard."

"I don't see any water on the court for me to drown in." Vikram laughs, turning his back to us as he dribbles his ball.

Ignoring him, I shake my head a little defeatedly at Halima. "I'm not actually a junior lifeguard yet. I've missed a bunch of classes because Nisha's spelling bees are at the same time. I'm missing class right now, actually."

"Don't feel bad. It kind of sounds like a pointless class," Vikram says, shooting his ball into the basket. "Unless you plan on being a professional lifeguard."

I grit my teeth. What is this kid's problem? He's like a fish louse, clinging to one cyprinid, determined to bring that fish down to make himself feel better.

Halima kicks a small rock across the parking lot. I can tell she is getting as annoyed with Vikram as I am.

"There's more to being a junior lifeguard than just saving drowning people. You actually learn all sorts of first aid stuff," Andrea replies, speaking up on my behalf again. "My swimming teacher was telling me all about it last year before I quit swimming."

I smile awkwardly, the insides of my lips scraping against my braces. I wish I spoke up for myself the way all these kids, most of whom I barely speak to, easily do on my behalf. Maybe I do need to start spelling things out for people. But there is a reason I never do the spelling bee. There is a reason I am usually in the audience and never onstage, speaking into a microphone while my voice is amplified one hundred times for an auditorium full of people to hear. I dig my shoe into the parking lot tar.

"You learn how to pull someone out of the water if they're drowning and lay them on their back," Andrea continues, "and check if they're breathing by putting your ear near their mouth and nose and seeing if you feel air on your cheek. Right?"

She looks at me, and I nod, sort of embarrassed by all the attention.

"It's neat. And important," Andrea adds firmly.

"Still sounds kind of funny," Vikram says with a snort, shoving a few more gummy worms into his mouth. "And if they're not breathing, you know what's next, right? Mouth-to-mouth. Blech." Vikram gags dramatically, and my ears burn. "You have to put your mouth on all those manikins everyone else does CPR on to practice. Slobbering on their faces where everyone in line before you already drooled? Now that's *actually* gross," he says, looking pointedly at Halima for calling him gross before.

I bite the inside of my cheek, feeling the soft part of my flesh against the wire of my top braces. It isn't gross. It isn't gummy worms purposely jammed in braces. It's how we learn. Coach Simone showed me the right way to tilt a head and do CPR with that manikin if they're drowning. I wish Vikram knew this. I wish someone else would tell him so he'd stop making fun of it.

"They're cleaned with alcohol." Halima huffs.

"Yeah," I add softly, as Sakura shoots a three-pointer, clearly not wanting to be part of this conversation with Vikram anymore.

"We should test your lifeguard skills," Vikram says, looking over at the gray fence next to us. "You know that one lady's house has an aboveground pool in it. You can watch us swim in it."

Akshay shakes his head. "No way. That's the woman who spoke up at the town hall meeting about the community center and said it shouldn't be renovated and should be torn down instead."

Ren's eyes widen, and he quickly stops dribbling. "The one who said she heard South Asian women pee on the grass before they build things to make it holy?"

I cringe, remembering how embarrassing it was when the paper covered that story and people in school talked about it. That woman even went on the local news. Aai says she was making up ridiculous stories because she didn't like the noise from the community center right in her backyard, which I guess would be annoying. I wouldn't want to have to listen to Vikram making other people feel uncomfortable and unimportant all day. But she could have made her point a different way, rather than spreading racist lies.

"That's the one." Vikram grins, throwing a big wad of gummy worms into his mouth as he rushes to the fence. "Come on." He runs his hand over the wooden pickets. "Hopping it is easy."

I watch Vikram stick his foot in a notch in the fence and feel my stomach drop as he gets halfway up the picket and peeks through the fence.

"Whoa!" he exclaims. "The water looks amazing. And it's hot today. Besides, don't we sort of need to get even with her after she said all that bad stuff about us?"

"So what are you going to do, pee in her pool and prove her right?" Halima asks, with an exasperated groan.

"You're so gullible." Vikram laughs, waving a blue-and-red gummy worm around before dropping it in his mouth. "I'm not going to do that. But

I do think I could jump in and do a lap around her pool and get back over it before she notices."

Sakura raises an eyebrow at Andrea. Are they feeling the same nervous feeling I'm feeling? Like an ocean is churning in their belly? Like something really bad is going to happen if we don't stop him?

"No, you can't," Ren says.

"Watch me," Vikram replies, popping more worms in his mouth.

He scales the fence, and everyone else rushes over to watch him, so I do too, not wanting to go against the tide.

But this *is* a time to go against the tide. Someone has to put a stop to this. You never get into a pool without a trusted grown-up around. That is Swimming 101. The first thing you learn. Well, that and don't pee in the pool.

"Time me," Vikram says, his cheeks looking like they are ready to burst from the worm convention in his mouth.

"I don't like this," Halima whispers.

I clench the wooden planks of the fence, my

palms sweating as I spot glimpses of the yard through the slats. It is empty. No grown-ups around. Not that it would be better if the woman who hates the community center in her backyard was there.

I'm not a certified junior lifeguard yet. But I know this is unsafe.

I clear my throat as Vikram swings his right leg over the fence. He is really doing this. He is actually going to trespass in someone else's yard, possibly get in big trouble for swimming in the pool or worse, and endanger his life in unsafe swimming conditions if someone doesn't stop him.

I look at the other kids. They're staring at him in shock, mouths open, with no sounds coming out.

Someone has to do something.

And it looks like that someone is me.

"Stop!" I shout, surprised at how loud I can get. Was I baleen-whale-loud?

Vikram yelps, startled, and falls back off the fence. "You fell for it." He laughs, covering his awkward dismount. "I can't believe you fell for it," he continues, laughing even louder, so loud a gummy worm falls out of his packed mouth.

I watch it practically slither on the ground in a puddle of saliva as Vikram continues to snicker at me. My ears burn. I had finally spoken up, and now I'm the butt of his joke. *Remind me never to do that again*, I think, when Vikram's giggles suddenly turn into coughing.

I look at him as Ren quickly bends down by his side.

"You okay?" he asks.

Vikram smiles, getting to his feet, coughing and laughing more, until suddenly there are no more laughs or coughs. And his skin starts to turn almost as red as Aai's tikli.

"He's choking!" Halima says.

My heart pounds in my chest. He is choking. Vikram is choking. I think back to what Coach Simone had taught us with the manikins. She didn't just show us how to save someone who was drowning with them. She also showed me exactly where to hit someone's back or do abdominal thrusts if they were choking on food. She even taught us how to help a choking baby with a baby-sized manikin, since that's a totally different method.

I look at Vikram and really *think fast*. I think about exactly where Coach Simone had showed me to use the heel of my palm on someone's back before doing abdominal thrusts.

"Help him!" Ren shouts, looking at me as Vikram motions toward his own throat and the red in his cheeks start to turn slightly bluish.

Without giving it a second thought, I spring into action.

"Hurry!" Akshay pleads, his eyes welling with worried tears.

"Get the parents!" I shout. "Get help! I'm going to start first aid."

Sakura and Akshay rush past me to the community center.

I stand to the side and just behind Vikram. I put one arm over his chest for support, help him bend at his waist so he is parallel to the ground, and then start to give him five back blows behind his shoulder blades with the heel of my hand.

"One," I say, huffing. "Two, three," I say, louder with each count. "Four," I cry, desperate for the food to get dislodged from Vikram's throat. "Five!" I shout, determined, smacking his back once more.

A wadded-up gummy worm ball goes flying out of his mouth like a flying fish, landing on the concrete. And Vikram takes a gasping breath of air, the color returning to his cheeks. He coughs hard and then sputters some words my way, but I can't understand them.

"You okay?" I ask.

He nods, taking in a few breaths of air. "You saved me," he repeats, clearing his throat. "You actually saved me!"

The community center doors swing open, and a mass of parents rushes toward us. I spot Nisha and my parents along with Priyanka Auntie.

"Do we need a doctor?" Andrea's dad asks from the crowd.

"I'm a doctor!" Sandeep's mom calls out, making her way forward.

"I'm a doctor," Nora's dad says.

"Me too," several other aunties and uncles in the crowd chime in.

I step back as the doctors check Vikram and his parents swarm him.

"What happened?" Aai asks, running to my side, Nisha and Baba right behind her.

"That kid over there, Vikram, he was choking," I sputter, my heart still racing from what has just happened. "I used what I learned in lifeguard class to help him."

Baba's mouth drops. "You did?"

I nod, wiping away tears of relief from my cheek as Nisha hugs me.

"Arey wah!" Priyanka Auntie exclaims, nearing us. "I'm so proud of you!" She raises her hand, going in to rub my head.

I duck back. "I actually don't like when you do that," I say softly.

Priyanka Auntie stops just short of messing up my hair. "What?"

I take a deep breath. I surprised myself with my whale voice when Vikram was going over the fence. And I was sort of impressed with it when I was helping Vikram when he was choking. I like the sound of it. I want to hear more of it.

"I don't really like when you do that to my hair," I say again, louder.

Aai and Baba look a little taken aback.

And Priyanka Auntie looks totally shocked. "Oh my god. I'm so sorry, betu. Thanks for letting me know. Fist bump?"

I smile. I am down with a fist bump. I offer my fist and she bumps it.

"Then this is our new way of saying hi." Priyanka Auntie beams. "If it's okay with you, that is."

I nod. Then someone taps my shoulder.

I turn to see Vikram standing there with his parents.

"I just wanted to say thanks," Vikram says softly.

"No problem," I say, over the hum of the crowd.

"You saved his life," Vikram's mom says.

"You're a hero," his dad adds.

"It was just something I learned in lifeguard class," I say, feeling my cheeks grow hot from the attention.

"Well, it was incredible," Vikram's dad says.

"Yeah, I might even sign up for your class with you," Andrea says from behind them.

"That would be fun," I reply. I look at my parents, who are beaming proudly at me and my lifeguard skills when they should have been at Nisha's spelling bee. The bee was interrupted, but there is something I still need to spell out. Even if it is in front of everyone. I clear my throat.

"Aai? Baba? Can we talk?"

I feel eyes on us from all around. Aai and Baba get a little closer, and I don't feel the stares anymore from the crowd.

"I know our family is into spelling bees," I start, as people begin to turn away. "I like cheering

Nisha on. But . . . I also really like lifeguard class. I love learning the first aid stuff and how to help someone if they're drowning or if they're choking." I take a breath and look at both of my parents, everyone else around us blending into the background. "It's important to me."

"I think it's important to Vikram, too," Nisha says, shoving her head in between my parents.

"Nisha!" Baba says, turning pink as a couple of the parents around us laugh. They must have been listening in.

"I mean, she's right," Vikram says, grinning. I guess he heard, too. "No lie there. Your sister's funny."

"Yeah." I nod, turning back to my parents. "If class is at the same time as another bee, not Scripps, but, like, a local bee, can I go? Maybe I can carpool with someone? Maybe even Andrea, if she starts taking the class?"

Aai nods, putting her arm around me. "We'll find a way to get you there. If it's important to you, it's important to us."

Baba joins in the hug, kissing my head. "Thanks for telling us."

It took me a while. But I'm glad I did. I smile. "Should we go back in?"

"I think they're going to restart the spelling bee," Nisha says.

My parents nod.

As everyone starts trickling back into the community center, I head in with my parents and Nisha, watching her confidently walk into the hall, chin up, ready to take on whatever comes her way. She is going to win today. It's pretty obvious. But I had a little win of my own today.

So, I hold my head up high too, thinking of getting to Junior Lifeguard class, thinking of getting certified, thinking of being able to help so many people and do what I love. Because thanks to my voice, I know I'm going to make waves.

OUT IN THE OPEN

by Rajani LaRocca

"VEDA, YOU'RE THE FEATURES EDITOR, NOT THE sports editor," says the editor in chief of the Maple Grove Middle School newspaper, brilliantly named *The Leaf.* Liam is an eighth grader, and he wears glasses and sticks a pencil behind his ear, just like they do in movies.

My chest feels like a pot that's about to boil

over, and my face feels like a flame. I try chewing on the end of my pencil, but it tastes disgusting, so I stop.

"I know that. I'm just saying I'm happy to help write about sports if it means the girls' teams get covered as much as the boys' teams. Last year's papers were very lopsided."

"Really? I don't remember that," Mike says. He's the actual sports editor and a seventh grader like me.

But I came prepared. I pull out the stack of last year's papers and plop them on the desk in front of me. "Only two out of last year's six issues mentioned anything about a girls' team. But boys' teams were in every single one."

We spend the next few minutes looking over all the papers.

"You're right," Mike admits.

"We definitely need to fix this. Great job, Veda," Liam says.

"I figured we editors should all start the year off on the same *page*," I say.

"Haha," says Callie, the news editor. "I agree, Veda."

"Girls' teams get equal coverage this year," Mike says. "I'll make sure of it when I assign the articles."

"Thanks," I say. It's amazing what can happen when you bring things out in the open. "I can help out if you want."

"Get me a list of your feature ideas before our big meeting next week, okay?" Liam says.

"Sure," I say.

"Meeting adjourned. Let's not miss the buses," Liam says.

I hoist my backpack on my shoulder and walk down the hall. Liam's more open-minded than the editor we had last year. And this year, since I'm no longer just a staff writer, but an editor too, he has to listen to my opinions, whether they're about features or sports or anything else.

That's what a journalist does. They observe and collect information. They analyze. And then they present the facts to give a clear picture.

I get to my school bus and can't help grinning.

I scoot in next to my best friend, Munia. "They listened. It worked!"

"Yeah!" she says with a smile that matches my own. We bump fists. Her fingernails are painted Radical Purple, and mine are Way Too Cool Blue. "Way to speak up, girl!"

"Your voice was whispering in my head the whole time. Writing about stuff is easy for me, but saying it out loud is a lot harder."

"For sure," she says, giving my arm a squeeze. "But I knew you could do it."

We spend the rest of our ride discussing schoolwork and weekend plans. Just before the bus gets to my house, Munia says, "You heard about the community center, right?"

I shake my head. "I'm going there tonight to cover an art fair, and of course we have band rehearsal in a couple days. What's going on?"

"People are arguing about it. Whether or not to spend the money on all the repairs it needs. It might be closing."

That's a surprise. "Oh, wow, that would be terrible," I say. I've spent hours and hours at the center since I was little. My whole family has. We've attended birthday parties and dance classes, plays and band practice sessions, and every kind of holiday celebration possible. "I guess if it does, we can alternate band practices at our houses?"

"We should do something about it," she says. "We can't let the center close." Munia acts like we can right all the wrongs of the world. And most of the time, I'm right there with her. But this feels like it might be too big for us.

"I don't see that there's much we can do," I say. "We're just kids. We don't have that kind of power."

Munia frowns, and we arrive at my stop.

"I'll text you later." I stand.

"Yeah," she says, but I can tell she's still thinking about it as I walk down the aisle.

My house looks calm and peaceful from the outside, but once I step inside, I'm assaulted by noise.

My brothers, Varun and Gautam, are playing *Mario Kart*. The volume is turned up so loud that I hear every acceleration, every screech, beep, and bell in the game. But their whoops and shouts are even louder.

"I'm home!" I call to them as I drop my backpack in a corner of the kitchen and look for a snack. Mom won't be home from work for a while, but she always leaves us plenty to eat.

I look in the fridge and spy some upma and tomato gojju. "Want a snack?" I call to my brothers.

No answer.

"Do you want a snack?" I yell.

"Nah, we're good. Get him!" comes Varun's deep rumble. It's so weird how over the past year his voice changed so much that now he sounds like Dad.

I heat up the food in the microwave, get myself a glass of water, and sit at the kitchen table. I grab my notebook, block out the video game noise, and jot down some ideas for features:

* Art Show at the community center—tonight!
* Chess Club
* Young Activists—talk to Munia
* Halloween Dance
* New menu/dining options—do they use real cheese in the grilled cheese?

I scoop a spoon of the upma and gojju and savor the contrast of fluffy grains and chunky tomato, salty and sour, spicy and sweet. If only the food at school was anything like this—maybe then I'd eat a real lunch and not be starving every day when I get home. I scrape up the last bits of food from the bottom of the bowl and continue working on the list as I sip my water.

An hour later, Mom and Dad walk into the kitchen.

"Hello, kanna," Dad says as he kisses me on the cheek. "Boys! Turn it down!" he bellows.

The noise stops almost immediately. Varun and Gautam must have switched to headphones.

"How was school?" Mom puts down her bag. Her hair frizzes out of her ponytail, her face droops, and she sighs as she straightens her back.

"Good," I say. "We had an editorial meeting for the paper, and I'm putting together a list of potential feature articles for the fall."

"My smart girl," Mom says, smoothing my hair behind my ear. "You must be hungry. Did you eat something?"

I nod. "Upma and tomato gojju. So yummy, Mom. You could bottle that gojju and people would line up to buy it."

"It's only delicious because it's made fresh and *not* from a bottle." Mom chuckles. "Do you want more?"

"Don't forget tea, Meena," Dad says as he heads for the stairs.

"Yes, yes, I'll make it now," Mom says. "It will be ready soon."

"I'm fine, Mom. I'm going to read in my room.

Could you take me to the community center later? There's an art fair starting at six that I'd like to cover for the paper. I should be done by seven."

"I need to take your brother to karate soon. If you get Daddy to take you, I can pick you up when you're finished."

"Okay, I'll ask him."

Mom washes her hands in the sink, then sets milk and water in a pan to heat on the stove before she rinses the dirty dishes and puts them in the dishwasher. Her whole body slumps. She looks so tired that I hesitate in the doorway.

Is she always like this? How have I missed it?

"Mom," I say.

"Yes, kanna?"

"I can help you make the tea."

"That's all right, Veda." Mom shifts on her feet.

"I'm helping." I walk back into the room and move her away from the stove. "Now tell me what I need to do."

"The milk!" Mom cries.

I turn to the stove, where the pot has started to boil over.

"Got it." I grab the pan and take it off the heat, but some milk bubbles onto the cooktop. "Shoot!"

Mom springs into action. "It's okay. Turn the burner off for a moment." She grabs a wet sponge and wipes up the spill, then puts the pan back on the burner. She relights it and turns the flame down low, just a flicker against the steel of the pan. As the milk returns to a low simmer, she grabs a box of loose tea and quickly scoops in a few spoonfuls.

"Mom, you're supposed to be teaching me," I say with a laugh.

Mom smiles. "It takes only a few minutes for me to make it," she says. "Do you want some?" Mom shifts on her feet again.

"No thanks. Was work tiring?"

Mom nods. "So many customers. So many who needed to return things. So many who didn't have receipts. I had to ask the manager for help twice."

"Why do you work there, Mom? It sounds awful."

Mom takes a breath and stirs the tea. It's turned a light khaki color already and smells amazing. "It's fine, kanna. This way we have a little extra to spend on the three of you."

"Yes, but why work in a department store where people yell at you and complain all day?"

"It's a job, Veda. It's all right."

"But you could do anything."

Mom's smile crinkles her eyes. "Not anything. My literature degree means I'm not qualified to be a computer programmer or an engineer or even an accountant, like your dad."

I think for a moment. No matter how long Mom's day has been, cooking always seems to bring her to life. "You're an amazing cook. You made dozens of kadubus for Ganesh Chaturthi. You made two hundred chapatis for last year's Diwali celebration. You should work in a restaurant!"

Mom shakes her head. "I do love cooking,

but restaurant hours are evenings and weekends, when you and Daddy and your brothers are home. It's okay, Veda."

"Meena!" Dad's voice booms from the living room. "Is tea ready yet?"

"Two minutes," Mom calls.

Mom grabs some pakoras from the fridge and heats them up in the toaster oven. "The microwave makes them soggy," she tells me. Soon she strains some tea into a cup, adds sugar, and mixes it, pouring back and forth with another cup in a milky ribbon.

"Give this to Daddy and ask the boys if they want anything," she says as she hands me the mug and the plate with the pakoras and homemade mint chutney.

I go into the living room, where Dad is sitting in his favorite chair with the paper open. He's reading the *Maple Grove Dispatch* now; next he'll tackle the *New York Times*. I hand him the tea and snack. "Thanks, kanna," he says.

"Dad, can you take me to the community

center at six? I need to cover the art fair. Mom said she can pick me up afterward."

"No problem," says Dad. "I'm looking forward to seeing your articles in here one day." He gives me a wink before he returns to the paper.

I head to the family room, where I find Varun and Gautam still playing their video game in the middle of a disaster area of candy and snack wrappers, cans of soda, and Cheetos dust.

"Hey!" I tell my brothers. "Mom's asking if you want a snack." Although, given all the wrappers, they shouldn't be hungry until tomorrow.

They ignore me. I know they're listening to their game, but they can still see me. Right?

I stand in front of the TV and wave my hands. "Hello?"

They don't even look at me. It's like I'm transparent.

I go to the wall behind the TV and unplug it.

"What the heck? Turn it back on!" Varun says. He just started high school and should know better.

"You ruined our game!" Gautam cries, and throws his hands in the air. He's in fourth grade and overly dramatic.

"Mom wants to know if you want a snack."

"Nope," says Gautam.

"Not hungry," Varun says.

"I know," I say. "But you need to clean up this mess. Mom's been working all day. You can't leave it to her to do it."

"You do it," Varun says, plugging the TV back in.

"Now we have to start that level all over again," says Gautam.

I fume as I start grabbing wrappers and cans. I refuse to make Mom deal with one more thing.

I take the vacuum cleaner from the hall closet and make sure to run into their toes as I vacuum up the Cheetos dust.

Something's got to change.

When Dad drops me off at the community center, I can't help glancing up at the brick building.

There were times when I felt annoyed at going to yet another dance performance or birthday celebration, but it feels weird to think this place might be going away now. I step inside and notice the worn tan carpet, the dull paint that's peeling in the corners. The building could use some love. But I'm here to cover the art fair, so I push those thoughts aside and head to the big room in the back.

I thought the art fair would be limited to paintings, but there are all kinds of talents on display, from abstract watercolors to ceramic animals to mixed-media collages made to look like portraits of people. The artists range from fourth grade up through high school. I interview middle schoolers and take lots of photos, hoping at least a couple make it into the paper.

It's seven before I know it. On my way out to meet Mom, I scan the community center bulletin board for upcoming events to cover for the newspaper. There are the usual flyers for babysitters, music lessons, and charity fundraisers. And then I find a notice:

ARE YOU A SOUTH INDIAN COOK?

I'd love to hire you for my catering business!

Please call Atiya Hayat for more information

732-555-8173

I rip off a tag with the phone number and press it tightly into my hand as I walk to Mom's car.

"Kanna, do you mind if we stop by Kaju's on the way home? I've run out of tamarind and cilantro."

"Sure," I say as I climb inside. "And speaking of food, I've found something interesting." I tell her about the sign and show her the tag. "Don't you think that would be perfect? You'd get to cook, but you wouldn't need to follow restaurant hours."

"Hmm," says Mom. "We'll see."

"We'll see" from Mom often means "no," but I bite the inside of my cheek to stop myself from talking. Maybe if I give Mom some time to think about it, she'll warm up to the idea.

We park in the small strip mall where Kaju's Indian Groceries is located. It's not much to look at, but it's always neatly organized despite being busy, and the spice-filled air is full of ingredients just waiting to be cooked. I think of how stirring pongal or payasam for hours never tires Mom like her current job, where she's yelled at all day.

We grab a basket and walk down the aisle for the tamarind paste first. I find the brand Mom likes and put it in the basket. We pass big bags of dal, rice, and smaller bags of whole spices on our way to the little produce section at the back of the store. There's the usual selection of Asian eggplants, various chili peppers, okra, cauliflower, and some weirdly shaped vegetables that I don't know the names of. Then comes a shelf full of herbs and greens: paalak, methi, mint, and more. Mom grabs two big bunches of cilantro and inhales their fresh aroma.

I continue our conversation from the car as we walk back to the front of the store. "What do you think, Mom? Wouldn't it be fun to try something else? Something to do with cooking?"

"I don't know, Veda. It might not be enough

work. It might be too much." She grabs a bag of raw peanuts and tosses it into the basket.

"You won't know that unless you call Ms. Hayat," I say. "Will you call her?"

"I don't need another job," Mom says.

"It's just a phone call to learn more," I say.

Mom caresses my cheek. "Okay, persistent one," she says. "We'll see."

We join the long checkout line at the front of the store and eye the refrigerated display of sweets. "Can we get some cashew burfi?" I ask Mom.

"Yes, if you'd like some. Are we celebrating something?"

"Kind of." I feel like getting her to even consider changing her job is something to celebrate.

A petite woman wearing jeans and a pale pink kurta with a patterned dupatta enters Kaju's, and the owner of the store, Mrs. Patel, waves at her. "I've got your boxes already packed here, Atiya. Do you need anything else?"

Atiya. And she's ordered lots of food—much more than for a single home. Enough for a caterer.

I throw Mom a glance, but she's looking at her phone and not paying attention. I tap her arm. "Mom, it's the woman from the flyer," I whisper. "The one who's looking for a South Indian caterer!"

Mom puts her phone in her purse and looks up. "What? Where?"

I tilt my head to Mrs. Patel, who's getting one of her assistants to bring boxes of ingredients outside. "Go talk to her."

"She looks like she's busy. There are too many people. And we're almost at the front of the line."

We put our items on the counter, and a cashier starts to ring them up. Atiya Hayat and Mrs. Patel are still talking. As Mom brings out her wallet to pay, I step out of line and put on my best reporter attitude.

"Hi," I say to the woman. "Are you Ms. Hayat? I'm Veda. I saw your flyer at the community center today—about looking for a South Indian cook."

The woman smiles, and her eyes are large and friendly. "Yes, I run a catering business and I'm looking for someone who can cook South Indian food. You know, dosas, idlis, South Indian curries. Sweets, too." She glances behind me. "Do you know someone who might be interested?"

"Well... maybe," I say as I look back at Mom, who's finished paying and is walking to me with her grocery bag slung over her shoulder.

I hold my breath.

What if Mom doesn't talk to her? What if she doesn't believe she should try to make things better for herself?

"I'm Meena Balaji," Mom says. "I'd love to hear more about the opportunity."

"Let's step outside for a moment," Ms. Hayat says to Mom. "I'll be back, Sapna," she says to Mrs. Patel, who nods.

Mom and I follow Ms. Hayat outside into the crisp fall air. The sun has set, but there's still a tinge of light blue on the horizon.

"My customers are interested in home cooking, and South Indian food is in high demand," Ms. Hayat says.

“I’m from Karnataka, and I prepare food from Karnataka and Tamil Nadu at home. But I can also make specialties from Andhra and Kerala,” Mom says. “How large are your events?”

“We have anywhere from twenty to two hundred. I usually have about four weeks’ notice. In general, you would be working on your own, but we could collaborate as needed.”

“That sounds good,” says Mom. “Maybe we can talk again this weekend to go over more specifics?”

“Yes, how about tomorrow morning, say at eleven? Here’s my number.” She hands Mom a business card. “You can also join me on a trial basis for a couple of events to see if it works for you.”

Mom nods. My heart inflates, and I can’t wipe the smile off my face as we all walk back into the store. Mrs. Patel gives Ms. Hayat the bill, and she looks it over and passes her a credit card.

“There’s only one issue,” says Ms. Hayat. “But it’s potentially a big one.” The corners of her mouth tug down. “We might have to put things on hold depending on what happens with the community center."

"The Maple Grove Community Center?" I ask. Dread pops the balloon inflating in my chest.

She nods. "If it closes, we won't have as many catering opportunities. People will shift to hotels where they can't bring in outside food. Then I won't be able to hire anyone new. It might be hard to stay in business myself."

"Our business would also suffer if the community center closes," Mrs. Patel says. "Atiya is a wonderful customer and caters so many events."

"Ah, I see," says Mom, and her smile falters.

During dinner that night, I put on my editor hat again and say what's on my mind. "So, I spoke with my editor in chief today about making sure that the girls' sports teams are getting equal coverage in the paper."

"That's cool," says Varun, startling me. "They should."

"Right," I say. Is this actually my brother?

"Candy Coleman is the best soccer player in our entire school," says Gautam.

"Wow," I say. "I had no idea you were both so woke."

"It's not about being woke," Varun says. "It's about being fair."

"So, that brings me to something else I wanted to talk about," I say, willing my voice not to shake. "About fairness here. At home."

I want to take photos of the puzzled expressions on the faces of Mom, Dad, and my brothers and stick them on my wall for when I'm feeling down. I bite the inside of my mouth to keep from breaking out in hysterical laughter.

"You mean, too many rules for us kids?" Gautam looks at me with his round brown eyes.

"Not exactly," I say.

"What's unfair at home, Veda?" Dad asks.

I take a deep breath. "Mom's doing too much on her own."

"Veda—" Mom starts.

"Hold on. Let me finish," I say to her softly.

"Mom is the only one who cooks and cleans anything here, *and* she works all day at a job she hates."

"I don't—"

"Please let me finish," I say. "I'm as guilty as anyone else. I don't help Mom with the cooking, and I complain if she asks me to pick up anything that isn't mine... or even if it is mine. And I kind of expect there to be food around all the time, even when she's not home. But it's not fair for her to work all day and then come home and work the rest of the day here."

"Is this true, Meena? Are you unhappy?" Dad looks at Mom like he's genuinely puzzled.

"I'm not unhappy," Mom says.

"But she's not *happy*," I say. "Her job drains her, and then she comes home and works even more."

"What do you propose we do?" Dad asks. "Should I learn how to cook? It's a little late for me."

"Well, Dad," I say slowly, "it's not too late, but I'm pretty sure Mom actually enjoys cooking. But we can help out with picking up and keeping things clean, right?"

No one says anything. Our house hasn't been this quiet since before Gautam was born.

"I'm sorry we made such a mess of the family room today," Varun says.

"What mess?" Mom asks.

"Veda cleaned it up before you saw," Gautam says.

"Thank you, Veda," Mom says.

"That's acting responsibly," Dad says.

I take a deep breath. "And Mom and I found out how to address the job problem, too."

"What job problem?" Dad asks, furrowing his brow.

"Mom's job is horrible. She deals all day with people who are awful to her."

"Veda, I already told you it's fine," Mom says.

"Tell them what we found out today," I say.

"Veda," Mom says. "I'll talk to Daddy later."

"There's a caterer looking for a South Indian cook," I say.

Dad looks at Mom.

"It's true," Mom says. "Atiya Hayat runs a

successful catering business and is looking for someone like me."

"You'd be interested in doing that?" Dad asks.

Mom nods. "I'm talking with her tomorrow. I think I'd love it." She puts her hand on my arm. "And I only learned about it because of Veda. She found the information, and when Atiya was there at Kaju's tonight, she made me talk to her."

"If it will make you happy, of course you should do it," Dad says as he squeezes Mom's hand. Then he reaches over and squeezes mine, too.

We celebrate with cashew burfi for dessert. Then I stand and address my brothers. "Come on, guys. It's time to clean up."

And to my surprise and delight, they listen.

Now I've just got to make sure our community center stays open.

Easy, right?

The next day, Mom talks more with Ms. Hayat, and she likes what she hears. She and Dad agree that the money would be good enough, and she'd be doing something she loves. It could work. If only Ms. Hayat was sure she was hiring.

I told Munia that we don't have any control over whether the community center closes. That we especially don't have any power because we're kids. But I think of all the hours we've spent there—socializing, competing, and celebrating. I hope the community remembers this.

But I'm a journalist. I can help them remember.

I'm going to collect the facts, analyze them, and present them to give a clear picture.

I text my best friend: "I've been thinking about the community center. I've got an idea, and I need your help."

The next day, Munia, Varun, Gautam, and I put up flyers. We start in the town center and end up at the bulletin board of the community center:

ARE YOU A KID BETWEEN AGES 8–13?

DO YOU USE THE MAPLE GROVE COMMUNITY CENTER?

I'D LIKE TO INCLUDE YOU IN MY ARTICLE!

PLEASE CONTACT VEDA BALAJI

vbalajijournalist@ymail.com

That afternoon, Munia and I meet our two other friends for band practice at the center. We use a small room tucked in a corner to rehearse. The room is worn and fraying at the edges, and the fluorescent lights make us look washed-out. But it's ours. Our place to explore and play.

We come back to my house tired but happy and order Chinese food for dinner. Munia, my brothers, and I watch a new Netflix movie and laugh our heads off. Miraculously, my brothers pick up after themselves without me reminding them.

Three days later, I have over a dozen emails.

I contact all the kids who responded and arrange interviews.

Then I write my article.

When I'm done, I think this story might be bigger than *The Leaf.* So, I send it to the town newspaper, the *Maple Grove Dispatch*. I want everyone in Maple Grove to read it. I hope they print it. I don't know if they will, but I have to try.

A day goes by, and I can barely pay attention at school. I check my phone in the hallway and at the end of every class, but the email I'm looking for isn't there.

Another day passes. No response.

I get home from school on Friday afternoon and check my email again. I find one that starts "Dear Ms. Balaji, we are pleased to tell you..."

My story runs in the *Maple Grove Dispatch* the next Monday:

AT THE CENTER

by Veda Balaji

The Maple Grove Community Center was built in 1978 as a "place for all to gather, in brotherhood and community." Over the years, it has been a place for people from a variety of backgrounds to assemble,

to debate, and to celebrate. It's been a place to hold public forums, host competitions, screen movies, and display art. More recently, different communities have held everything from traditional holiday celebrations to baby showers and religious rites, in small groups and large. My own family is there almost every weekend.

What will happen if we lose our center? I decided to ask some of the people who are most affected but have the least power to keep the community center open: kids. Here are some highlights from what they had to say.

Eleven-year-old Sanjay said, "The Maple Grove Community Center is like an octopus with a bunch of different arms for all the different things everyone likes to do, from spelling to language classes and everything in between. But it's also like an octopus because all those arms can sometimes work together to lend a helping hand or lift someone up, because that's what a community should do."

"We have birthday parties and Chinese New Year celebrations there," said ten-year-old May. "It's a fun place."

Jashan, age twelve, noted, "I like the center and I have a lot of friends there through the programs I've attended and the classes I've taken."

Nine-year-old Oliver said, "I like the art classes. I get to use pastels. It's better than at school."

"MGCC is a multilayered biryani, a place where all the flavors of South Asia come together to form a cohesive dish," said thirteen-year-old Duaa.

And twelve-year-old Munia summed it up like this: "Maple Grove means a place where all of us belong. Maple Grove means community and home."

The Maple Grove Community Center needs refurbishment, and that takes money. When we think about what's worth spending money on, we should consider the

voices of the kids in our community—kids to whom this place is much more than a building. It's a place where they compete, dance, make music, eat, and cheer. A place where they laugh and cry and everything in between. Through the years, this center has meant so much to so many, to those who've lived in our community for years as well as those who've just moved here. And right now, for my South Asian community in particular, which is so varied and diverse, it truly is a center—a place where all of us can come and feel we belong.

It's the first time a student from Maple Grove Middle School has gotten an article into the *Dispatch*. Liam, Mike, Callie, and the rest of the newspaper staff go crazy, and we have a party to celebrate at our next meeting.

Mom and Dad have bought almost thirty copies of the paper, and they won't stop talking about it to everyone they know. It turns out that many adults care about the community center, too—especially when they realize what it means to their kids.

Mom smooths my hair and cups my chin in her hand. "No matter what happens, I'm proud of you," she murmurs.

"But what if we can't do it, Mom? What if we can't save the center?"

"Then we'll find other ways to gather," she says with a smile. "No one can keep us apart forever."

"But what about you? What about the catering job?"

"Even if the catering job doesn't last, I know I can't stay at my current job. I'll find something else. Daddy says he supports me in whatever I want to do. You've shown me that I need to investigate more possibilities."

"I have?"

"Yes, kanna, you have." Mom pulls me into a hug.

Even though we don't have money or power, kids can do something when we see something wrong or unfair. We can notice. We can gather facts and tell others about it. We can encourage everyone to care and to speak up. And maybe, just maybe, we can help make a change.

It's amazing what can happen when you bring things out in the open.

ANSWERED PRAYERS

by N. H. Senzai

ONE NIGHT, WHEN MY MOM WAS IN AN UNUSUALLY talkative mood, she told me a secret. In a quiet voice, she revealed that she'd married my dad only a month after meeting him.

A month? Wow, I thought, but kept it to myself. This was a story I needed to hear.

She went on to tell me that they'd first met at a café at the University of Miami, where they'd both gone to school. Her eyes sad, she said that she'd been amazed that the gorgeous guy, the one all the girls crushed on, was interested in her. Four weeks later, they were sitting across from each other, flanked by their parents, having tea at her house. His family proposed marriage, and although her parents thought it was a bit rushed, she'd said yes. Six months later, they married, graduated from college, and moved to New Jersey, where my dad got an engineering job with a Japanese electronics company.

For the next three years, seven months, and twenty-eight days, Mom prayed for a baby. Then, for two hundred and eighty-one days, she prayed for a healthy baby. And in honor of those endless prayers, my mom had named me Duaa, which meant "prayer" in Arabic. However, during those long days and nights, those prayers had not been my mother's only ones. . . .

* * *

"Duaaaaa!" calls a voice from near a towering archway, assembled using multiple shades of violet, lilac, and silver balloons.

I snap out of my thoughts and get up from behind the buffet table where I've been pinning up skirting. On the table beside me, Mr. Pandey is setting up his AV equipment, muttering to himself as he checks his phone for the hundredth time.

"Do you need any help?" I ask. Last week, at the Sinha wedding, he'd misplaced his connector cables and I'd had to track them down.

"Uh, no thanks, Duaa dear," he says, eyes magnified behind thick glasses. "I need to step out for a bit. An emergency at home."

"Duaa, where are you?" repeats Bally as Mr. Pandey scurries out the door.

A lean figure in a snappy navy suit and matching turban, Bally pauses a moment to adjust a misaligned place setting, causing his long manicured beard to whip through the air as he pivots left.

"I'm here," I mutter, squeezing out from between the table and the wall.

"My dear," he sighs, eyeing my black jeans and dark gray hoodie, emblazoned with GAMES. THE ONLY LEGAL PLACE TO ANNIHILATE STUPID PEOPLE. "You really can do better. With a few wardrobe changes and a haircut, you would be radiant, darling. Just *fierce*."

I snort, having heard this suggestion for the third time from him in an equal number of months. The last time was the Malik engagement party at the Glenview Golf Club. I have no desire to be radiant or fierce. Except for maybe when I'm online with my gaming trio and fiercely taking out the competition.

"Well, I'm just trying to be helpful," Bally says with a playful wink. "Now, back to matters at hand," he continues, waving his arm across the sprawling space.

I blink, taking in the entire effect for the first time. After six hours of hard work, the room is unrecognizable. I've seen Bally decorate this same room, the main hall of the Maple Grove

Community Center, many times, but today, his genius is in overdrive. The peeling paint, water stains, and shabbiness is glossed over with sumptuous lengths of chiffon. Tables are artfully draped in crisp linens and set with fine china and silverware. The focal point of each is a towering centerpiece, filled with flowers. For the first time, I wonder what the event is for—I haven't been paying attention since I wasn't even supposed to be here. Maybe it's a doctors' convention of some sort. Mom catered a gastroenterologists' gathering last year at a posh country club that needed a vegan menu. Bally had created an entire digestive system using flowers—weird but pretty realistic.

"Speechless?" Bally asks triumphantly. "I'm used to it."

"It looks fantastic," I agree, cracking a begrudging smile.

"Tell your mom we set up the chafing dishes for her," he says with a wave as he heads out the door, his troop of designers, painters, and florists behind him.

With a deep sigh, I trudge across the wooden floor, scuffed and filled with scratches from long years of dance recitals, birthday parties, weddings, plays, political campaigns, and scout meetings. I've helped my mom at what feels like a hundred events at the community center. And on most days, I was usually happy to help. But not today. I feel my face shifting into what my mom calls DDG—Duaa's Dour Glower. I wear the title with honor and even chose DDG as my screen name.

Right now, I can't help it. At 9:25 a.m. this morning, I was fine-tuning my PC. First, I cleaned the keyboard of crumbs and then washed my mousepad. I needed to get used to my higher-sense mouse since it allows for better reflexes. The better the reflexes, the less likely you'll get killed. I was ready, and so was the rest of my team, who I met online last year. Slick, who shares a birthday with me, is in Atlanta, and Raptor lives in Toronto and is a year older than us. Within a week of meeting, we'd clicked and joined forces. After months of preparation, we'd ended up qualifying for semis at the Troid annual tournament.

I still can't believe we made the top three hundred teams from North America East. We'd gotten a hundred and forty-two points, even though we died off spawn in the fourth game. It had been an unlucky game that ended up putting us behind. We had to refocus and get our act together. With Slick and Raptor at my back, I picked it up.

Usually, I was as sure-footed as someone doing parkour and we popped off on the seventh game by getting a seven-kill dub. On the eighth game, we placed third, and if we make the top twenty in the finals, we have a shot of making good money. If I kick butt, I could even sign with a gaming org and get paid to play. That's why today was so important. It was the first day we were all free to prep hard and focus on mechanics. In particular, we needed to coordinate our game sense.

Right about now, I probably would have been taking a break to eat a slice of cheese pizza with pineapple and jalapeños—the snack of champions. Mom also saved me half a dozen mini red velvet cupcakes, leftovers from what she'd baked for our neighbor's baby shower.

Then, at 9:26 a.m., and again at 10:47 a.m., two of my mom's regulars called in sick. All of a sudden, she was shorthanded. And even though Mom hadn't asked me to work tonight, I realized I had to. I'd seen the desperate look on her face. It's a look I'm familiar with. One that I hate seeing. So here I am, in a role I'm often in: Ms. Fix It, Clean It, and Wash It. A regular Duaa of all trades.

I head down the hall, past a giant board plastered with help-wanted signs, dance lesson reminders, Girl Scout meeting schedules, ads for various tutors for math and science, and a flyer announcing an upcoming Save Maple Grove Community Center rally and fundraiser that Mom and I plan to attend. Skirting around decorations for a Halloween party the following week, I push open the double doors to the kitchen, my ears assaulted by the clang of spoons and pots, grumbling from the dishwashing station, and muffled curses from burnt fingers. I look for my mom and find her at the stove, stirring a huge pot of chicken tikka masala. She raises her other arm, as if it's a conductor's wand, and waves it vigorously, encouraging the rest to speed up.

"Everything going okay, ladies?" she asks, a booming voice coming from a tiny woman with long hair piled on the top of her head, covered in a hairnet. She paces in her impossibly high platform heels, which I toppled in whenever I used to try them on as a little kid.

A chorus of yeses breaks through the din. Except one. A tentative arm goes up. It's Mrs. Balaji, the mom of Veda, the girl who'd pestered me for a quote for an article she was writing on the community center. At first, I found her pushiness annoying until I realized that the story may help keep the community center open. Veda and her mom came over last month, carrying Tupperware filled with aromatic South Indian dishes. I loved the delicate, fluffy idli served with yummy coconut chutney, accompanied by a hot and spicy soup called sambar. Mom had hired her on the spot.

After helping Mrs. Balaji, my mom heads toward me, holding a box. "Everything look good out there?"

"Pretty amazing."

"Bally is good." Mom nods in approval. "That impeccable taste of his got him that spread in *Bridal* magazine. Mrs. Jaffer was lucky to land him." She hands me the box, filled with burners for the chafing dishes. "Put these in. The last thing we want is to have cold food because we forgot to set this up in the last-minute rush."

While she heads over to attack the salad, I slink back into the cavernous hall, maneuvering around the tables. I eye the towering centerpieces, admiring how Bally's florist managed to put so many shades of purple into one cohesive arrangement. There's eggplant, periwinkle, lilac, and a shade that looks like blueberry pie. I catch a whiff of lavender, the only flower I recognize.

Mom's client, Mrs. Jaffer, spared no expense

in trying to make the place look as luxe as possible. I know the old community center wasn't her first choice. Just last week, she'd given Mom a frantic call about a fire at the super fancy hotel she'd originally selected, which allowed outside food. Since its ballroom was shut for repairs, she'd been scrambling to find a new location. As I sat at the dinette table doing my homework, Mom suggested the community center. At first, Mrs. Jaffer had scoffed. "That run-down old dump?"

I'd bristled like a porcupine at her tone. Sure, the community center isn't fancy, but it's where my mom does a lot of her business. Unfortunately, Mrs. Jaffer wasn't the only one with a negative view. There have been calls for the center to be defunded, even shut down. But after contacting over a dozen venues, Mrs. Jaffer found out that it was the only option left on short notice.

Just as I place the last burner in the chafing dish, I hear footsteps heading toward the main doors to the hall. A woman in a flowing purple and silver dress enters, enveloped in a cloud of strong perfume. She calls out to those behind her, and I recognize her voice from Mom's earlier phone calls. It's Mrs. Jaffer. A man in a suit and tie struggles in with a trolley piled high with boxes, and right behind him is a boy. A flash of heat radiates down my neck. It's him. Sal. Sal *Jaffer.* The lights flicker in my brain, and I connect the dots. Sal reigns over the seventh grade, along with the rest of his squad, Tiffany, Daniel, and Padma, commonly known as the popular kids.

Sal is the captain of the soccer team, the lead in the school play, and the head of the robotics club, and his grades aren't shabby, either. I've been in his class since the beginning of the year, and he and his friends still don't know I exist. But then again, I want it that way. To keep out of their line of sight. I have no desire to be associated with a bunch of snobs. Without realizing what I'm doing, I dive behind a table as if I were evading a necromorph, a freakish mutated corpse in the sci-fi game *Dead Space*. Not that I'm allowed to play *Dead Space*, since it's rated eighteen. I'm only allowed to game at all because I promised Mom that school and grades come first.

And because of those grades, Mom insisted that I apply to Sumter Academy, where I'd gotten a full scholarship to attend. Despite a lot of grumbling that I wanted to stay in my public school, I'd agreed to go when I saw how happy it made her. So now I wake up an hour earlier, wear an itchy navy uniform, and take two buses to go to a fancy-pants school that prepares young ladies and gentlemen for success. A school Sal has attended since kindergarten. A school where I feel like a necromorph who's landed in Candyland, so I basically keep my head down and focus on my work.

I'm not the wishing type, but at this moment I do make a wish—for a cloak of invisibility or ring that would help me disappear. Out of habit, I squeeze my eyes shut. Behind my lids, memories come flooding back...memories of when I was around five years old. I can practically hear the front door open with a familiar bang. I jump up from the floor and shove my dad's toolbox, which I wasn't allowed to play with, back in the cupboard, and run. I find my favorite hiding spot and squeeze in between the washer and dryer. I melt into the shadows, away from the echoes of shouting, slamming doors, and breaking dishes.

"Thank God, it looks better than I thought," I hear Mrs. Jaffer marvel in relief.

I open my eyes and peer around the corner, watching her wander around the room in wonder.

"People shouldn't care what it looks like," mumbles her husband. He shares an exasperated look with Sal and adds, "It's for a good cause, after all."

Mrs. Jaffer ignores him and hands Sal a sheet of paper. "Salman, follow the seating chart and put these on each table. Make sure the mayor is at the head table."

"At your command, mother jaan," he says. He saunters off to set up white and silver signs, cursive writing listing table numbers and the names of various organizations: Sridhar and Patel Family Law, St. Benedict Health Clinic, Sikh Family

Center, Asian Pacific Institute on Gender-Based Violence, Crescent Mosque, Johnson Family Foundation, Safe Space Therapy, and the YWCA of Maple Grove. A tingle runs down my spine as I recognize many of the names. This is definitely *not* a birthday or engagement party.

Mrs. Jaffer stands near the podium, staring at her watch. "Where's the AV person? He should have been here an hour ago."

I glance over at the table Mr. Pandey had been setting up. It looks halfway done. Exactly the way he'd left it when he rushed out. Before she can say anything else, Sal's dad returns with another load of supplies, followed by a group of elegantly dressed women.

"Uzma," calls out a tall woman with a shock of red hair. "We came early to help."

"You're a godsend, Melissa," gushes Mrs. Jaffer, going over to give her an air-kiss and hug.

I notice that Sal is preoccupied with a tall, retractable banner. *Time to leave.* Trying to be as invisible as I can, I slide out from around the table and make my way to the kitchen. One of the women who's just arrived stands between me and the exit. I just need to make it around her, and then I'll be home free. Head down, I hurry past, catching a glimpse of short white hair and a magenta shawl over plump shoulders. In my rush to exit, I miscalculate the space between her and the table.

"Goodness," she gasps as I step on her foot.

"I'm so sorry," I garble, grabbing her elbow. *How can I be so clumsy IRL when I'm so graceful in the virtual world?*

I look over her shoulder and catch Sal staring. He blinks in recognition. *No hiding now.* I jerk my gaze away.

"It's all right, my dear," she says.

Startled by her voice, I look up.

"Duaa? Is that you?" she asks, peering into my face.

I nod, astonished. "I'm so sorry, Freny."

"Nothing to apologize over, dear. Lucky that I wore my sturdy boots."

I grin. Today's turning out to be one surprise after another.

"I knew your mom was catering tonight, and I was looking forward to seeing her and eating her delicious cooking," says Freny. "Running into you is the icing on the cake."

I stand there, wishing that I could disappear. I've always been awkward around people, even those I like. I guess you can chalk it up to being an only child, one who didn't get out much. *Get a hold of yourself*, I scold myself. I actually love Freny, and a small part of me is thrilled to see her. But it also brings back glimpses of a life I'd rather forget.

Freny gently takes my hand and maneuvers me to a table. I stare into her warm brown eyes; the same eyes that had shown my mom and me so much kindness four years ago. She'd been the answer to my mother's third greatest prayer.

"How have you been?" she asks.

"Fine."

"How is school?"

"Okay. I transferred to Sumter this fall."

"Now that's a good school." She smiles. "Are you still a whiz at fixing things?"

I nod, hiding a smile.

"I still tell people about my electronics genius who fixed all the timers and the sprinkler system."

"I didn't really fix the sprinklers," I say. "I just rebooted the system to its original setting and it started working again."

"Well, whatever you did, the lawn and garden haven't looked so good since!"

There's a pause. That weird moment when no one speaks and there's an awkward silence.

"How is your mom doing?" she asks.

"Really well. Her business has taken off and people love her food." I add, "Though she's worried about the community center being shut down."

"Yes, I've heard all the ugly news," says Freny. "There is a lot of anti-Asian sentiment going on right now."

I nod, about to tell her about the rally when a voice interrupts us.

"Freny, how have you been?" It's the red-haired woman, Melissa.

As the women chat, I look down at the agenda sitting on the plate.

5:00	Registration
5:45	Welcome by Dr. Uzma Jaffer
6:15	Award ceremony: Freny Yazadi
6:30	Keynote speaker: Mayor Samuel Pratt
7:00	Dinner and fundraiser
8:00	Tabla and sitar ensemble

The pieces come together. I look around and catch a glimpse of purple in every nook and cranny of the room: flowers, banners, and various hues in the clothing worn by the guests. I spot the banner Sal has finally unfurled.

AWARENESS + ACTION =
SOCIAL CHANGE.

HONORING DOMESTIC VIOLENCE MONTH

It dawns on me why there is so much purple splashed everywhere. It's the color adopted by the domestic violence prevention movement. Pressure builds in my chest. Without saying goodbye to Freny, I bolt. On the way to the kitchen, I sneak into the bathroom and lock myself in a stall. As I press my clammy forehead against the cold tiled wall, the memories come flooding back. Of my mother's second greatest prayer, which had not been answered, no matter how much she pleaded and begged.

After I turned eight, five years ago, Mom and I snuck out of our house in the middle of the night. Our possessions were stuffed in a small suitcase packed with essentials: identification cards, important papers, and the money she'd saved over the previous six months. Mom had come to the realization that no matter how much she prayed, Dad wouldn't get better. He wouldn't stop getting angry, throwing things, not letting Mom visit her family and friends, and not giving her enough money to buy groceries and necessities.

On that dark night, Mom drove on the highway, something she rarely did, to a small apartment complex. She'd buzzed at the gate, and Freny invited us in with open arms. After a snack of cookies and milk, she'd shown us to a studio apartment, hung with bright pictures and a welcoming throw on the pillowy bed. The next morning, I'd learned that we were in a shelter for victims of domestic violence. This had been my mom's third duaa: to be safe and free.

The following week, we met Chandni Sridhar, the lawyer representing Mom in the divorce. Mom thought Dad would fight and play dirty, but he'd surprised us all by turning into a wimp. After he realized we weren't coming back, he quickly signed the papers and gave full custody of me to my mom. He moved back to Miami, and just last year he remarried. My mom made a duaa for the poor woman who is his new wife. Now, besides an occasional phone call, where he doesn't have a lot to say, or a birthday card with a check, I don't hear from him much. And I'm fine with that. Mom and I needed a hard reset in life. Like you do on a computer—press down on the power button and reboot.

I take a deep breath and count backward and think about a happy moment, the way Emily from Safe Space Therapy had taught me. I close my eyes and imagine being on the battlefield with my trio, racing up the hill toward victory. I suck in a cool, deep breath and open my eyes. As I think about tonight, and what the event is about, I'm actually glad to be here. To honor Freny and the other amazing organizations that help people. People like me and my mom who prayed for safety and a new chance at life. As my nerves calm down, a loud crash sounds down the hall. It's from the kitchen. I run.

Fifteen minutes later, I'm calmer, the old memories tucked away in a file and placed in a secure spot in my brain. Nothing like getting busy in the kitchen to get your mind back on track, and I've nearly finished cleaning up the fallen salad when

Mrs. Jaffer bursts in, her eyes a little wild. "Can you serve dinner now?" she cries.

Mom looks up from chopping a fresh batch of cucumbers. "What happened?" she asks.

"The AV guy. He's disappeared," sputters Mrs. Jaffer. "The equipment is not set up, so I can't start the program. Guests can start dinner while we try to find him."

"No problem," says Mom. She calls out instructions, and the ladies begin piling the trolley with steaming trays of food. I run ahead to light the burners under the chafing dishes as the crew lays out the spread of delicious food. The room is packed, and the guests look a little restless. As I put out the salad and Mom places the dressing beside it, Mrs. Jaffer grabs a glass and a knife. Mom and I move back toward the AV station as a sharp clinking echoes through the room, followed by a hush.

"Welcome to our annual gala! We look forward to celebrating how your awareness and action bring social change to the issue of domestic violence,"

Mrs. Jaffer's voice rings. "Our program will get started shortly. Meanwhile, please begin dinner." She puts down the glass and begins to guide the crowd toward the buffet table.

"Atiya," a warm voice calls out. It's Freny.

Mom stops what she's doing and gives her a huge hug, and they fall into conversation.

"Has anyone seen Mr. Pandey?" asks Mrs. Jaffer, heading toward the AV table, which is being quizzically stared at by her husband, Sal, and half a dozen uncles.

"No one's seen him," says Mr. Jaffer.

"We need to get this set up," she hisses, waving her hand over the equipment.

"Don't look at me," says her husband as Sal shrugs.

"Anyone?" asks Mrs. Jaffer.

Two men politely look over the system, shake their heads, and wander off to dinner.

"Javed," Mrs. Jaffer says, turning to a portly uncle in a rather tight suit. "You're an engineer. Can you fix it?"

"I'm a civil engineer, my dear. If it were a bridge, I'd fix it in a jiffy." He guffaws at his own joke.

It's a good thing Mrs. Jaffer already put down the knife. But if looks could kill...

I have to say something. I take a deep breath and blurt out in a rush, "Mr. Pandey went home. He had an emergency...he said he'd be back."

Mrs. Jaffer looks at me as if she's seeing me for the first time. "Why didn't you tell me?"

I mumble, "I thought he told you."

"Call him again, Sal," she says.

Sal gives me a sympathetic look and presses redial. But after two tries, Mr. Pandey doesn't pick up.

"Oh Lord, help us," Mrs. Jaffer whispers a prayer.

"Duaa," my mom says with a pointed look. "You've helped Mr. Pandey before."

I need a mental buff—a nudge to make me more confident. I take a deep breath and think back to the day my trio and I had fought our way into the semifinals. I remember that feeling—that I could do anything. *I can do this.* I put my game face on and step forward.

"Uh," I mumble, heading toward the equipment. "I can take a look at it."

Mrs. Jaffer doesn't look very convinced. But she's out of options.

I inspect the equipment Mr. Pandey had managed to put together, and it looks like it's in the right order.

"Can I help?" asks Sal.

I look at him, tongue-tied.

"You're Duaa, right?" he asks. "Started school this fall?"

I nod, not quite believing he knows who I am.

"I, uh, tried to talk to you. Twice," he says. "Both times you kind of ignored me and walked off."

I dissed him? Unbelievable. An uncomfortable knot settles in my stomach.

"I'm, uh, sorry about that," I say. "Being in a brand-new school has been a bit confusing."

He nods as if accepting the pathetic excuse. "I know you're new and all, but there are cool people at Sumter," he adds.

Maybe I'm the one being a snob? The thought blows me away. But I don't have time to think about it.

I switch the subject. "We need to make sure all the cables are secure." I hand him a blue wire and point to the back of the projector. "Find the slot behind the screen and plug it in."

As he follows my instructions, I connect the remaining cables. I check the sound system. I open the control panel and press the test button. After hearing a reassuring beep, I move on, running through the rest of the checklist.

"Can you see if the visual display is on?" I ask Sal while I fiddle with the back of the monitor.

Sal peers at the screen and shakes his head.

The monitor is on, but the screen is black. The computer is asleep. I say a little prayer and hope a simple wake-up call will work. It's an easy solution that's often overlooked.

I shake the mouse on the pad and hold my breath. Sal looks over my shoulder and lets out a whoop as the lights flicker and the system purrs to life. I hand Mrs. Jaffer the mic.

"You can start the event now," I say.

"Thank you, my dear!" she gushes in relief, and pins the wireless mic to her shirt. "Salman, I need you at the podium," she adds, and hurries off with a file of notes.

"That was awesome," says Sal. "You really should talk to Mrs. Peterson in the theater department. They could use your skills for sure."

"Yeah, maybe," I say with a smile.

"And next time, say hi back," he adds before running off.

I sit down to run the AV system, still amazed that someone at school knows that I exist in the real world. I play the intro music, alerting guests that the program is about to begin.

Mrs. Jaffer stands at the podium. "I hope you are enjoying the lovely food, prepared by Lazeez Catering," she says, and the room fills with murmurs of agreement. "Before I begin, I want to say a special thank-you to the young lady who came to our rescue tonight." She points toward the AV table.

I freeze as hundreds of curious eyes turn toward me.

"Duaa fixed the AV system and saved the night," she says.

The room fills with the echo of clapping, and my cheeks turn the color of raspberry jam. But strangely, I don't want to hide under the table this time. It feels nice to be the answer to someone's prayers, the way Mom knew I'd be.

TOGETHER AT THE CENTER

by Hena Khan

"YOU KNOW NOBODY'S SHOWING UP AT SIX O'CLOCK," Baba warns as he glances over my shoulder and points at the screen. I'm typing out the invitations for my party, sandwiched between my parents on the sofa.

"Don't worry," Mama says. "I'm adjusting for Desi Standard Time. Dinner won't be served until eight."

"Dinner?" I ask. "I thought the party was supposed to be lunch. Remember?"

Mama shakes her head. "It's dinner. I already booked the hall and spoke to Atiya Auntie about catering."

This is the first I'm hearing about *any* of these details.

"Catering what?"

"A nice buffet. We can pick out whatever you like. Butter chicken, channa, you name it. But definitely biryani. And some kind of korma."

I guess we're having desi food.

"What happened to pizza?" I wonder aloud.

"Oh. We'll have pizza too, for the kids. And a big cake from that new bakery on Maple Lawn Drive."

Baba shoots me a worried look, and I exhale slowly. At least one of my parents understands. This party sounded like a blast when we first talked about it a few months ago. My ameen. Celebrating that I've finished reading the entire Quran in Arabic after six years.

I'd imagined a big cookout, with carnival games. But now it's turning into just another fancy, boring dinner party. I signal my father to say something to Mama, and he nods at me with a look that says, *I got you.*

"Doesn't this all sound a bit..." He pauses and clears his throat. "I don't know... *expensive*?"

Wait. *What?*

I suddenly realize that he's not worried about the same thing as I am at all.

"Mama," I interrupt before she can respond. "You said this was going to be a *fun* party! I thought we were going to get a photo booth. And a bounce house for the little kids."

My younger brother, Azaan, comes running into the room when he hears "bounce house."

"Yes!" he whoops. "Can we get the one with the basketball hoop that Jacob had at his bar mitzvah? It was so awesome! I could dunk on it!"

Mama sucks her teeth.

"Halima," she begins, resting her hand on my shoulder. "This is a big moment for you. We're so proud of your accomplishment. But that's why this should be more formal, a classy event. Remember when the Jaffers had their ameen for Salman? Wasn't that nice?"

"You mean that over-the-top thing at the country club?" Baba snorts. "It must have cost as much as a wedding!"

I remember Sal's party. I sat at a kids' table in the corner, bored during speech after speech by Sal's uncles and dad. The highlight was whispering with my friends Maha and Rahma, scarfing down gulab jamuns, and trying not to giggle when everyone was hushed. I forgot that it even was an ameen, because whatever the cost, it also *felt* more like a wedding than a kid's party. Everyone was super dressed up, and there were silver tasseled boxes with gold-wrapped candies inside them at each place setting. I still have mine in my room.

"I know the community center isn't as nice, but

I'm going to see about a decorator. I've heard about this great guy named Bally," Mama continues.

Baba and I exchange looks again, and now even I'm worried about how much this is all going to cost. I'd *much* rather spend money on hiring the hypnotist who came to my friend Andrea's birthday party than some fancy decorations to cover up the old walls at the Maple Grove Community Center.

"What about entertainment?" I ask.

Mama smiles brightly and puts her hand on my back.

"That's you, my love. *You're* the entertainment. Everyone is going to listen to you read from the Quran. Your favorite passage. Sister Lamis can help you practice."

I almost laugh before I realize that my mother is dead serious. And as she starts to go over the ridiculously long guest list with Baba, filled with a bunch of names of people I don't even recognize, it's clear that there's no room for arguing with her. If Baba can't get her to remove any of the extra people, I won't be able to convince her to get a photo booth. She has this party all figured out. But it suddenly feels like it's more for her than it is for me.

"Those who struggle get the most reward," Sister Lamis always told me when I'd get frustrated during my Quran lessons. And it's been a struggle all right. I began when I was about six years old, sitting at the kitchen table every Sunday while my grandmother-like teacher with a warm laugh taught me the letters of the Arabic alphabet.

She'd give me stickers that I put on my folder when I did a good job and alternated between calling me "habibti" and "sweetie." Slowly, I learned how to connect Arabic letters, which change shape depending on if they are in the beginning, middle, or end of a word. After I mastered that, I began to read short words from a special booklet.

But that was just the beginning.

After almost two entire years of prep work, I was finally ready to read the Quran, at the age of eight. Sister Lamis made a special duaa, and then I started, haltingly, with her correcting me, line after line. After months, I could read an entire page. Then I worked my way up to getting through a few pages in an hour.

"There are people who devote their entire lives to learning how to read the Quran, memorizing it, and reciting it perfectly," Sister Lamis would remind me when I would get frustrated by the vowels that live *outside* the letters, or the many rules about what gets pronounced or stays silent or gets extended in Arabic. Sometimes she'd play me samples of experts reciting the Quran on her phone to inspire me. They always sounded a bit echoey, like someone recorded them in an empty marble mosque. But it was beautiful, and we'd munch on the snacks Mom put out while we listened.

"Not 'ah,'" Sister Lamis would gently correct me as I read. "It's 'aaaaah.'"

When it came to certain letters, like "ein" or "haa," she patiently had me repeat the sounds after her, over and over. After a while, I thought I was getting pretty good at it. But the pinched skin between her eyes as she exaggerated the sounds told me I still wasn't there yet.

Sister Lamis is from Syria. She speaks Arabic, and she understands the Quran. My family is from Pakistan, and we speak Urdu. Urdu's got some words that are like Arabic. And the alphabet is similar. But that's about it. That's why our parents hired Sister Lamis—to make sure that Azaan and I learn Arabic properly.

Some kids I know raced through the book, finishing by age seven or eight, which made me feel like I was behind. Even my younger cousin Rehan finished when he was only nine. But I went extra slowly because Sister Lamis would stop me after a few verses to explain the meaning of what I had just read. My parents insisted on that, saying that I needed to understand the lessons of the Quran, and not just recite the words, even if that meant I didn't complete it until I was twelve.

The best part of my lessons was when I finished reading and could sit back and listen to

Sister Lamis tell me stories of the prophets, of Nuh and his big ship, Yunus trapped in the belly of a whale, and Muhammad and his patience during hard times. Each time, Sister Lamis would end with "And that is why it is important to be good, and to be nice to your brother, and to take care of your parents when they are old just like they take care of you now." I'd glance over at Mama at those moments if she was in the kitchen, listening as she often did, and catch her nodding her approval. I can't help but wonder if my parents made a deal with Sister Lamis to get her to drill that message into me as much as possible.

Today, I thumb through my worn Quran as I take a bite of the chocolate-covered dates Sister Lamis gave me as a congratulations gift last Sunday. I'm looking for the passage I'll recite at the ameen. I'll practice until I can sound it out without any mistakes. The idea of standing in front of everyone and reading aloud makes my heart beat faster. But when I imagine my teacher's and my parents' faces in the front row, filled with pride, my nerves are overpowered by a whole lot of joy.

I just need to find the perfect passage to recite.

"Rehan? As in *my little cousin* Rehan? Are you serious?" I sputter.

"Yes, Halima." Mama continues to chop onions and doesn't look up. "You're overreacting. It isn't that big a deal."

But oh no. She's wrong. This *is* a big deal.

"It's supposed to be *my* special moment, isn't it?" I ask. My mother keeps saying that at least, even though as the day gets closer, it feels like it less and less. If that's even possible.

"Of course it is." Mama says it like I'm a five-year-old.

"Then why does *he* have to be a part of the program? Let him have his own party," I grumble.

"Come on, Halima." Mama frowns. "Don't be like that."

I fume in silence.

Mama sighs, wipes her hands on a dish towel, and turns to face me.

"You can share the stage, can't you? You know how hard he's been working on his recitation for so many years. It's so beautiful."

I know about it, for sure. I've been hearing about my perfect cousin Rehan and his Quran skills for years. I hold back a groan because it's probably wrong to react that way to the idea of someone reciting the Quran. But Rehan is just so . . . smug. And to be fair, it's not like all that reading of the Holy Book makes him *act* any holier or anything. He's still mean to his older sister Rania and me when we visit. He still hogs the TV and whines when it's our turn on the PS4. And he *never* shares his candy.

Mama continues to gush about him anyway.

"He didn't get to have an ameen, so it would be nice for him to have the chance to recite in front of everyone too, don't you think? And we can recognize him, too."

I think back to when Rehan's grandfather

suddenly fell ill in the spring. He and Rania missed school for three weeks to go to Cairo because it looked like it was the end. But then his grandfather recovered, and the family returned, relieved and thankful, with armloads of presents for us. But Rehan's ameen was canceled and never rescheduled.

Rehan's mother is my mother's sister. And his father is from Egypt. Rehan's been hearing Arabic his whole life and visiting Cairo almost every year. So it makes sense that he recites Arabic so well. He's half Arab after all. But no one seems to remember that, or the part about there being more reward for those who struggle. He has it *easy*, and that still doesn't stop him from being braggy or super annoying.

It doesn't help either that all the aunties are obsessed with him and his big eyes, dimples, and curly hair. It's disgusting. But Rehan loves the attention, basking in the cheek pinches, smiling through all the praise, and eating up all the treats the aunties pile on his plate at parties. They act as if all that Quranic training has left him weak and in need of extra nourishment.

"I'm sure Sister Lamis would be thrilled to see two of her favorite students on the stage together, reading from the Quran," Mama adds. "You can do that for her, can't you?"

It's like she's been saving my teacher as her secret weapon. What am I supposed to say?

"I'll think about it" is all I can manage. "But Rehan's name isn't going on the cake." Mama took me to the bakery last week to try cake samples, and I picked chocolate with white chocolate icing.

Mama smiles and squeezes my shoulder.

"Thank you, for thinking of everyone else," she says, like the matter is settled. But I still don't like the idea of Rehan worming his way into my event one bit. And the thought of him biting into my cake with that superior look on his face leaves a bitter taste in my mouth.

Baba slams a copy of the newspaper onto the kitchen table.

"Look at this," he mutters. "Thirty years living in this city, and I never expected to see something like this."

"What is it?" Mama asks. She stops washing dishes and comes toward him. I quit emptying the dishwasher and follow her.

"It's just so infuriating!" he continues, running his hands through his hair.

I check out the paper, the *Maple Grove Dispatch*, and don't see anything but ads for a used car dealer and a law firm for personal injury.

"Increase in Car Break-Ins," a headline reads.

"That's terrible," I say.

"No, this." Baba points. "I mean, yes, that's terrible, too. But look at this letter."

It's a letter to the editor. In response to a recent article. I scan it quickly.

"This person is arguing that Maple Grove Community Center should be closed instead of renovated," Baba explains as I read. "They want to divert the funds to build a new dog park."

"We've heard about that debate for a while,"

Mama says, sounding unsurprised. "The city council is going to vote on it."

"I know, but listen to these reasons this person gives for closing the center." Baba pauses and then reads from the paper. " 'Noise pollution, traffic issues, loitering, strong food odors, unauthorized vendors.' "

"Hmmm." Now Mama frowns, too.

"What?" I ask, confused.

Baba looks at Mama, who nods her head. Then he looks at me and sighs.

"It sounds like people who oppose the center don't like some of the things it's used for. Or maybe even the people who use it," Baba says.

"Does it say that?" I glance back at the paper.

"Not in so many words," Baba says. "But if you read between the lines. The center is heavily used by people of color, immigrants and others, for our parties and cultural classes and programs. Like your ameen."

"So?" I ask, trying to stay calm and act mature, even as a tiny prick of fear pierces my chest.

"So, that threatens some people. They don't

want to see us practicing our traditions or our culture. They don't like the smells of our food, the sound of our music, or how we pray."

"Oh." The prick in my chest intensifies to a pinch. "Am I still having the ameen, then?"

Baba takes the paper and drops it in the recycling bin, and then he turns to give me a hug.

"Of course you are. We rented the hall, and we have every right to celebrate this occasion the way we want."

Mama forces a smile and turns to me.

"What was that you wanted before? A photo booth? Maybe we should look into that?"

"Yeah," I mumble, but I'm still thinking about the letter.

Why would anyone have an issue with our food, or prayers, or anything else?

It just makes no sense.

Sister Lamis adjusts her scarf and takes a sip of her coffee. She puts another spoonful of sugar in it and stirs.

"Go on, sweetie," she says.

I continue to recite the passage I'm thinking of reading at the ameen. My teacher listens, corrects me a few times, and, when I'm finished, nods her head.

"Very nice," she says. "Read it a few more times and you will be ready."

"Are you sure?" I falter. "I was also thinking of a different surah."

"It's up to you, sweetie," Sister Lamis says, reaching for a biscuit. "Which one do you want?"

That's the problem. I don't know what I want. I mean, I want to find the passage that speaks to me and captures the spirit of the event. And one that I know well enough to recite nicely and keep people's attention. I found a few possibilities, but I can't choose.

"Can I try this one?" I ask.

"Of course." Sister Lamis smiles.

I recite the new passage, but I'm distracted and mess up, reading the same line twice.

"Not that, start here, habibti," Sister Lamis corrects me.

I fumble through the rest of it and then stop, exhausted.

"You will do fine. You know it," Sister Lamis soothes, reading the worry on my face. "Just relax. Do you know what it means?"

I read the translation before and have a rough idea. But I still like the way Sister Lamis explains things the best, so I say, "You can tell me."

I chew on a biscuit and try to concentrate while she talks, but my mind wanders. A bunch of thoughts swirl in my head, and one of them is Rehan and how he can probably read any page of the Quran without even practicing and how impressed everyone will be by him. *Annoying.* Then my thoughts turn back to the letter in the newspaper and the idea of people not liking our events, even something as nice as the ameen. It makes my face flush with anger, and I try to focus again while Sister Lamis keeps talking. At the end of her explanation, she turns to look at me.

"So, be a good person, and remember God, and be kind to your brother, and listen to your parents, and be good to them like they are good to you."

There it is. I smile and nod. But then Sister Lamis surprises me.

"So, after your ameen, are we finished with our lessons?" she asks as she picks up her mug again.

"What?" I ask, swallowing the bite of the biscuit I just took.

"You finished the Quran, so are we done? For many of my students, after the ameen, we stop reading together."

"I don't know." I pause. I can't imagine not seeing my teacher every week. She's become a big part of my life that I don't want to let end. "Maybe we can start over?"

Sister Lamis smiles into her cup and grasps my hand.

"Of course, habibti. I just wanted to make sure you want to. It will be easier for you next time. You will be faster, insha'Allah."

I don't remind her about getting more reward for struggle, because she looks so confident. But

I'm pretty sure it will still be plenty hard for me next time around.

Mama and I pull up to the community center to check out the banquet hall and decide how many tables to set up inside next week.

When we walk into the lobby, there's a small group of people hanging up posters that read COMMUNITY MEANS U AND ME and ALL ARE WELCOME HERE and DIVERSITY MAKES US STRONGER. They're old and young and a mix of races.

I hear a little catch in Mama's voice as she leans over and says, "Look at that. That's the Maple Grove I know."

As we stand there, watching them, I realize they must be reacting to the letter in the paper that Baba showed us, and to the fight over the community center. Suddenly, an idea pops into my head. I turn to Mama.

"How about instead of having the party the way we were planning, we turn it into an open house, for anyone who wants to come?" I ask.

Mama nods thoughtfully. “Are you sure, meri jaan? You really want strangers there?”

I don’t say that she’s already invited a bunch of aunties and uncles I don’t know. So really, what’s a few more strangers?

“If they want to come, that’s good, right?” I ask instead. “I don’t know if it will, but maybe this can help. If people who feel like they don’t know people like us can come to the ameen, talk to us, and eat some biryani, I’m sure they will love it. And if not, there’s dessert.”

Mama’s eyes grow wet. She doesn’t say anything but pulls me into a big hug and kisses the top of my head.

Back at home, we’ve returned to planning mode.

“That’s really what you want?” Mama asks me. “Instead of getting the photo booth?”

“Yeah. And we can lose the flowers, too. I don’t need them.”

Mama pulls up her party planning document. It’s a spreadsheet with tabs. And very organized. I can tell that my coming up with changes just as we were about to send out invitations is stressing her out a little, but she's doing it anyway.

"I guess we can shorten our guest list to make extra room," she says as she squints at the names.

Baba looks at me pointedly.

"That's an excellent idea," he agrees.

Azaan tugs on my sleeve.

"I don't get it, Halima," he pouts. "Why aren't you getting the bounce house? That would be so fun."

"It's going to be dark outside by the time the party starts," I say.

"There are lights outside on the basketball court," Azaan argues.

"It costs a lot of money," I whisper. "And we need to cut back now that there's going to be a lot more people coming."

"I think we can manage the bounce house and still open up the event," Baba says slowly. "Don't you think?"

"Yes!" Azaan cheers.

"Yeah, that'll keep the kids entertained," Mama agrees.

I guess that means I'm not the only entertainment anymore. But that's a relief. Now that the party has changed, I've been searching for a new verse to recite. And I think I've finally found the right one.

"We have no idea how many people will actually come," Mama says. "What if we run out of food?"

"We'll figure it out," Baba says. "And if we need to, we can always order more pizza."

Azaan turns to me and gives me a high five. Maybe this party will end up being fun after all.

I was a little worried that hundreds of extra people would show up, but it's more like thirty, which is perfect. All our family friends are here, of course, plus my friends from school. A few of our neighbors came, and a bunch of people I don't recognize. Some might be the ones who were putting up the posters the other day.

"This rice dish is so flavorful," a lady in a fleece half-zip with a Maple Grove Community Center logo sewn into it gushes as she comes up to the buffet for seconds. "What do you call it?"

"Biryani," I reply.

"Bur-ee-an-ee," the lady repeats slowly. "Delicious."

"It's got some kick!" the man next to her says. "Reminds me of a dish my mother made in Jamaica."

"The yogurt helps cut the spice," Mama says, pointing to the raita.

"Thank you for having us," the man says. "And congratulations to you, young lady."

"Thank you." I smile.

The man has a goody bag in his hand and holds it up like a little salute as he walks away. They aren't as fancy as Salman's, but we put some Hershey's Kisses and Hugs in little bags with a tag that explains the significance of the ameen and laid them out on a table by the entrance to the hall.

I survey the room, filled with groups of people

talking. Mama called the decorator and explained what we were doing, and instead of flowers, he offered balloon bouquets and moon and star garlands to cut costs. Those, along with twinkling lights, make the place look special. And even Mama seems satisfied that it's classy enough.

The bounce house is outside, along with a couple of parents who volunteered to monitor it. Baba came over a few minutes ago and told us that they had to pull out a bunch of big kids who were getting super rowdy and almost toppled it over. They're in the hall now, sweaty, searching for lemonade, in a mix of desi clothes and pants and shirts. Jeevan's wearing a bow tie that's sideways now, and he grabs a slice of pizza and nods at me. And there's Rehan, part of the pack, his fancy kurta all wrinkled now. He grins at me and chugs his drink and looks so happy I can't help but grin back at him.

His sister, Rania, is here, along with Rahma, Maha, Chaya, and Munia. Sister Lamis is in the corner, talking to one of Mama's friends. And Sal is talking to Atiya Auntie's daughter, Duaa, who I almost didn't recognize because she's smiling.

"Assalamalaikum, everyone," Baba says, tapping on a microphone that squeals so loudly that everyone drops their forks and covers their ears.

"Sorry!" He grimaces. "Thank you all for being here. It means a lot to us that we are all together tonight to celebrate Halima's achievement of finishing the Quran, masha'Allah."

Everyone claps and cheers and one of the uncles yells out, "Takbir."

All the Muslims in the room respond with a resounding "Allahu Akbar."

Baba smiles and nods, and then continues.

"We want to take a moment to honor her teacher, Sister Lamis, who's been working with Halima for the past six years. Halima, can you come up here, please?"

I take a deep breath and grab the microphone from my dad. Then I turn and face my teacher, who is seated at a table in the front of the room.

"Thank you, Sister Lamis, for being my

teacher. For being so patient with me since I was just a little kid. For making learning the Quran fun and for teaching me its lessons. I'm so grateful for you. And it's because of you that we are all here tonight."

Then I run and get a big bunch of flowers that Mama had arranged and a gift bag and hand them to Sister Lamis. She stands up, hugs me hard, and says, "I'm so proud of you."

"And now I'm going to read a passage of the Quran from Surah Al-Hujarat," I continue. "I'll read it in Arabic first and then explain the meaning in English. And then my cousin Rehan will read a passage that he picked, since he's been working hard studying the Quran too, and is really good at it, and because this is a night for all of us."

Then I begin to recite the passage in Arabic, paying extra attention to every letter. I remember when to elongate and when to pause and try hard to get the pronunciation just right. I trip up a couple of times but quickly correct myself and get through it.

"This passage is about community and how we treat each other," I continue, remembering Sister Lamis's words. She practiced with me over the phone until late last night. "These verses talk about being good to each other and not fighting. About how to make peace when you have a problem with someone. To not call names. To not make fun of each other. To not backbite. It talks about how God made us all different from each other. Into different nations and tribes. So that we can know each other. And depend on each other."

I look around the room and see everyone nodding, Muslims and non-Muslims, friends and strangers. It fills me up with hope.

"And it also says that no one is better than anyone else. And that God loves those who are good to each other the most," I conclude.

I glance at my mother and father as I say the last part and shake my head at Azaan, who has just spilled fruit punch down the front of his kurta. They are beaming, and my eyes fill up as I smile at them, and everyone applauds.

It's a struggle for me sometimes to remember to be good, to be kind, to be nice, and all the things that Sister Lamis has been reminding me about for the past six years. But I'm trying. I'm grateful that everyone is here together, including Rehan. And even though I thought I wanted a party just for me, it means more now that it's for everyone. If there's more reward for those who struggle, tonight feels like I got a lot, in so many ways. And I still haven't even had my cake yet.

THE MAP OF HOME

by Sayantani DasGupta

"MUNIA! WHAT A PRETTY NAME, DEAR!" SAYS THE substitute teacher, pronouncing my name like it's a lunar cheer: "Moon-Yah!"

The classroom smells like feet and Lysol, like markers and boredom. It's too early to have to deal with this, but here I am.

"It's Munia," I repeat, correcting the teacher with the right pronunciation: Moon-ee-ah.

"Well, that's not how it appears on the page," the sub says, like she's accusing me of tripping her up on purpose. "But how lovely and exotic!"

I groan softly to myself. Our normal teacher, Ms. Brandon, is out, and by the curious expression on the sub's face, I know the next question that she'll ask me. Because if there's anything I've learned during my twelve years on this earth, it's that folks like to locate people like me. Like I'm a pushpin to stick with the pad of their thumb into a map.

My best friend, Veda, gives me a *look* from her desk across the room, where she's sitting under a giant collage of Abraham Lincoln, Martin Luther King, and Malala Yousafzai. I'm not sure what the collage is supposed to represent, but I guess it's supposed to inspire us kids. Only, I don't feel inspired. I feel cornered and angry. Because, like Veda, I know what's coming.

And right on time, there it is.

The substitute teacher widens her green eyes and smiles stickily-sweetly at me, like I'm a dead butterfly she's examining under a magnifying glass. "Where are you *from*, dear?"

I feel my heart beating faster. I know the answer she wants, which is "India," of course. If I say "India," she'll be satisfied, and go on with roll call. If I say "India," the lesson will continue as expected, and the substitute will keep smiling, and the world will keep turning. If I say "India," though, I'll be lying. At least, kind of.

I take a big breath and meet Veda's eyes again. She nods. Malala and Dr. King look like they want to nod, too. Veda and I practiced this together at home. We promised we'd be brave and push back at those people who really just wanted to ask us: "Why are you brown?" and also "Why are you here?"

"Dear?" the substitute prompts, speaking louder and slower, like ridiculous people do when they think you can't understand English. "Where—are—you—from?"

Other kids in the room start to snicker. I feel the heat creep up under my skin. I clear my throat, putting on my bravery like it's armor.

"Ohio," I say softly. Then, louder, I repeat, "I was born in Ohio and then moved to New Jersey in first grade."

The teacher frowns, her face falling from delighted to frustrated in under a second. "No, dear, not Ohio. I mean, where is your *family* from?"

The lady's eyes are glittering with annoyance like she can't believe I won't just answer the question the way she wants. She wants my answer to be "India." I know it, and everyone else knows it, too. But Veda and I practiced. And I'm tired of these questions. I'm tired of everyone thinking people who look like me only belong in certain faraway places.

I take another deep breath, wishing the ugly, tiled floor of the classroom would open and swallow me up. Or, better yet, open and swallow the substitute up.

"My mom's from Massachusetts," I say,

my voice only a little trembly. "My dad's from England. They met in college."

As if I've really done something wrong, even more kids start snickering. The substitute teacher's eyes are about to bug out of her head. I have a flash of a memory, to driving on the Garden State Parkway and having some jerk lean his head out the window as he cut off our car, yelling, "Go back home where you came from!"

I had felt small and humiliated until Baba had leaned out too, yelling back, "I would, but London weather's rubbish, mate!"

The car guy had made a rude gesture, but his face was confused. Like he thought my dad was saying the city of London was in India or something.

Like that guy, my substitute teacher doesn't want to hear about Ohio, or Massachusetts, or England. She wants to think of spices, and elephants, and a place far away where brown people belong. A place not here in Maple Grove, New Jersey. And she wants that so badly, it makes her really angry.

"If you're going to be a smart aleck, young lady," begins the sub, and I feel my stomach drop with fear at what's coming at the end of that sentence. What's she going to do to me? Give me detention? Send me to the principal's office?

"India," I say, feeling dizzy with frustration and fury. The substitute's face relaxes into a smile as I say, "My family is from India."

I can't get over the sick feeling of disappointment all day.

"It's not your fault!" says Veda. "You tried!"

We're riding our bikes after school down to the community center, and on a normal day, I'd be whining about our upcoming band practice. It's Veda who's got the songwriting talent. I'm okay at playing the guitar but am way shaky when it comes to singing. Still, my best friend won't let me quit our all-girl band no matter how much I complain about not being good enough. "We're always the worst at seeing our own strengths," she says.

But today, I'm not even thinking about practice or my mediocre vocal skills. I'm still stuck going over the drama with the substitute teacher at eight that morning.

"I didn't try hard enough!" My voice cracks on the words. I don't know how to explain what I'm feeling, even to Veda. Even though she'd been there, encouraging me, even though we'd practiced at home, I'd still felt so alone and so powerless. "I wish racists weren't so bad at geography!"

Veda smirks. "Oh, come on. Maybe the sub just wanted you to offer her some chai tea brewed in the authentic way of our people."

"Or naan bread!" I snort with laughter, almost falling off my bike in the process. Veda knows just how to cheer me up. We're always laughing about how "chai tea" just means "tea tea" and "naan bread" just means "bread bread," but everyone just keeps saying it like that anyway.

"Or maybe she was craving a samosa!" giggles Veda. "Why do people always want to talk about samosas with us? I mean, it's not like anyone asks people of Scottish heritage about haggis all the time."

I frown, steering my bike around a bumpy piece of sidewalk. “What’s haggis?”

Veda smiles in that “I’m a journalist about to dump a bunch of knowledge on you” way that she has. “Oh, just sheep organs boiled with spices, onion, and oatmeal inside its stomach.”

“Just waiting for me to ask, weren’t you?” I’ve obviously walked right into that one. “You got way too much pleasure out of telling me that.”

“It’s my job to make sure everyone has all the facts,” my best friend chirps.

“Yeah, yeah, I know.” I roll my eyes, laughing. “Democracy dies in darkness and all that.”

We’re still laughing and joking around when we see it. The sign. Veda must see it at about the same time as me because she puts her legs down and stops her bike just as I do. And it’s not just one sign. It’s the same flyer taped up a zillion times, blanketing the community center fence. Obviously, whoever made the flyers didn’t have a limit on the number of copies they could make, like we do at school.

MAPLE GROVE IS AN AMERICAN TOWN!

BUT TOO MANY SNEAKY AND COMPETITIVE IMMIGRANTS ARE MOVING IN!

THEY'VE INVADED OUR COMMUNITY WITH THEIR RELIGIOUS RITUALS, LANGUAGE CLASSES, AND CRICKET MATCHES!

DEFUND AND SHUT DOWN MAPLE GROVE COMMUNITY CENTER!

HYGIENE STANDARDS AREN'T FOLLOWED AND THE CENTER IS FALLING APART!

KEEP MAPLE GROVE WORKING FOR REAL AMERICANS!

"'Real Americans'?" I echo, my voice sounding hollow to my own ears.

Veda sounds equally freaked. "What's that thing your mom always says about Asian Americans—perpetual something?"

"Perpetual foreigners," I say. My mom's a big-time activist who runs a women's shelter and is always lecturing me and Veda about different stuff. "That no matter how long we've been in this country, or how many generations, we're still seen as outsiders."

"Yeah," says Veda in a flat, hurt voice. "That."

"Who would put these up?" I get off my bike so I can go up to the fence and read the papers more carefully.

My heart is beating super fast, and I feel sweat trickling from under my rainbow-colored unicorn bike helmet all the way down my neck and back. I mean, my baba and all my desi community uncles play in those Sunday cricket matches! They're super boring and confusing to watch, but Baba loves them! And by "religious rituals" did the sign-writer mean the Durga Puja, Eid, and other festivals we sometimes have in the community center? I feel like whoever has written these signs is holding a super-bright spotlight right on my family and community, like they've drawn a big target "X" on our backs.

Veda looks as shocked as I feel. "I can't believe it! It's got to be some kind of joke!"

"It's not a joke, it's trash!" I start ripping down the flyers and crumpling them up. "I mean, 'sneaky and competitive'? That's just code for 'Asian' or 'desi'!"

With every paper I crumple, I feel all the anger I've stored up at the substitute teacher from the morning. Plus the anger I've kept hidden at rude racists on the parkway. I'm so angry at all the haters, I worry for a second that my fury will burn me right up.

"Wait, should we be doing that?" Veda squints at me. It's a bright, golden afternoon, and it's seriously disturbing how so much ugliness can happen under such a beautiful sun.

"Why not? Who's going to stop us?" I flip my black braid over my shoulder and keep ripping down flyers with my chipped-purple-polished nails.

"I don't know." Veda bites her lip. "This is a little bit more than standing up to a substitute teacher. What about free speech? Are we destroying private property?" Veda pauses. "Not that I'm a fan of Chief Justice John Roberts!"

I pretend-laugh in reply, because honestly, I'm not completely sure who John Roberts is. Veda's idol, besides intrepid woman journalist Nellie Bly, is Ruth Bader Ginsburg, and she's always making Supreme Court references that I really need to start looking up online.

"Why are you making up excuses for racists?" I ask her. "I thought that's what we decided we wouldn't do anymore!"

"I know." She nods. "I guess I just don't want the signs to be real, you know? And doing something about them feels like we're admitting that people hate us." Her voice chokes a little on the word "hate."

I stare down at my scuffed-up combat boots, kind of surprised at how emotional I feel, too. It's like all the little hurts from my whole life—screamers on the highway, people not pronouncing my name right, subs demanding to know what I am, like I'm not even human—are all piling up together and manifesting in this terrible flyer. And yet, why do I feel ashamed—like it's my fault that I'm brown?

As if reading my mind, Veda puts her arm around my shoulders and says fiercely, "You're right. Whoever made these signs, they're the ones who are wrong, not us!"

I nod, feeling silly for tearing up. Veda squeezes my shoulder with her surprisingly powerful fingers. For a small person, she really is very strong. "So, what are we going to do about it?" she asks.

"Why are you asking me?" I snort, rubbing at my wet eyes. "You're the idea person, Madam Journalist."

"Obviously my article about funding the center to stop it from getting torn down wasn't enough," says Veda grimly.

"Your article was amazing for raising awareness, but we've got to do more." I turn my attention to the crumpled papers in my hand. Maybe it's my turn now to do something. I can't fail, like I did that morning. "So, what do we do? We can't let these jerks shut down the community center!"

"Do what we always do when in doubt," Veda shouts in her best superhero voice, hands on hips.

"Burn it all down to the ground?" I'm only kind of joking. "Oh, please say we burn it all down to the ground!"

"No, silly." Veda points her finger dramatically to the sky. "Go to the library!"

To my relief, Veda agrees to delay practice. After calling the other girls in the band, we take ourselves to that bastion of learning—the Maple Grove Library, which is conveniently next door to the community center. Without showing Ms. Chandrashekhar, our favorite librarian, the awful flyers I maybe, possibly illegally pulled down, we start peppering her with questions.

"Wait a minute, young scholar-activists!" Ms. C. puts up her hands to stop our flow of words. She has like five pencils stuck in her messy bun and some wack-bright red glasses on, making her look like a rounder, desi version of Ms. Frizzle. "Are you talking about those flyers up around town that suggest shutting down the community center?"

Veda and I exchange shocked looks, but we

probably shouldn't be so surprised. I guess it had never occurred to us that we weren't the first people to have seen the flyers. Also, that there are more flyers around town than the ones we'd taken down from the community center fence.

"We might be," I say, trying to play it cool. "And if we *are*, we also might be trying to think of a way to stop whoever wrote them!"

"And save the community center!" adds Veda.

"And save the community center!" I agree, thinking of how sad Baba would be without his cricket matches. And where would my mother's women's group hold their fundraisers? Without the community center, where would we have spelling bee prep, or band practice, or Odissi dance lessons?

Ms. C. looks at both of us thoughtfully for a minute. Then she dusts her hands on her very funky periodic table of elements skirt, indicating we should follow her into the stacks.

"I would recommend that you think about what other young people have done when facing similar challenges," the librarian says as she hands us a bunch of books. "Remember, a lot of dedicated, visionary people came before you, and it would behoove you to learn from them, figure out what worked for them and what didn't." Ms. C. gives us a critical look. " 'Behoove,' in this context, means 'be incumbent upon.' "

"We knew that," says Veda defensively.

Ms. C. blows at a curly hair that has escaped her bun. "I never said you didn't," she singsongs before sailing away.

"Is it just me, or was her definition for 'behoove' more confusing than the word itself?" I mutter.

"Not just you," Veda agrees.

Veda and I sit down at one of the long research tables and start flipping through the books Ms. C. has taken down for us. "See?" I point to some racist cartoons from the early twentieth century, and then to one of the flyers, which we've uncrumpled to lie flat between us. One cartoon shows stereotypically drawn Chinese men trying to sneak into the country, only to be stopped by Uncle Sam.

Another caricatures Japanese people during World War II pretending to be loyal to America but then selling secrets to Japan. "I told you that 'sneaky' and 'competitive' were racist code words for Asian immigrants!"

"And look!" Veda points to a passage that describes how immigrants from Asian countries were blamed for bringing diseases like cholera and yellow fever to the U.S. "So is all that stuff about hygiene! As if the immigrant communities who use the Maple Grove Community Center are unclean, like we don't know how to keep the place disease-free and running well!"

I have a sudden, fiercely painful memory of Jimmy Pollan sniffing at me in the first grade and complaining that I smelled like "curry," even though that's not even a real desi food. I think of how ashamed I sometimes still am at the noise and chaos, not to mention tinfoil tubs of food, that my Bengali community produces when celebrating Durga Puja at the community center. Like how, even though I'm proud of being who I am, I'm always hoping that no non-desi kids from school wander by when we're unloading our cars.

"You young scholars may also find some articles of interest online!" says Ms. C. as she drops a list of search terms and links on the table in front of us. One of the pencils wobbles in her hair as she bends down, but as if she has a magic sixth sense, she jams it back into her bun again. "I've reserved you some time right now on both computers number two and three!" Ms. C. points at the library computers she's reserved for us before whirling away again to help other patrons.

Picking up our books, Veda and I make our way over to the computers and start searching around. I point at the screen as I read an article Ms. C. had suggested. "Look! This is about a town in California that just apologized to its Chinese residents for racist things it did in its past, like being a 'sundown' town."

"What's that?" Veda wrinkles her brow, leaning over to my screen.

I stare at the computer, skimming some more.

"Apparently, Chinese immigrants weren't allowed to walk on the streets after sundown. It's something that happened to African American people all over the U.S., too."

"Here's something else!" Veda jabs her finger at her computer, and I scooch toward her to see better. "In 1907, in Bellingham, Washington, a mob called the Asiatic Exclusion League attacked South Asians living and working in their community. Man, why don't we learn about any of this in school?"

I pick at my flaky purple nails as I keep reading out loud off the computer. "Post 9-11: Anti-Muslim hate crimes rise and affect other communities too, like a turbaned Sikh man named Balbir Singh Sodhi, who was murdered after the 9-11 attacks."

"This has been going on forever." Veda slumps back in her library chair.

I feel the anger inside me firing up again. I take in a big breath. "But there's no way people just sat around and took all this, right?" I think of my mom and all the fierce aunties in her organization. "We must have fought back?"

Veda looks back at my computer, "Hey, there's a movie here made by two high schoolers about some anti–South Asian incidents right here in New Jersey in the eighties by a group called the Dotbusters."

"Dots, like the bindis desi women wear?" I ask, my eyes getting bigger.

"Yeah." Veda nods grimly. "They apparently wanted to chase all the desis out of their town, and a bunch of South Asian people got beat up and terrorized. One Indian American man even got killed."

Veda and I share her set of headphones and listen to the short documentary. "Wow!" she says finally, as we watch a crowd of brown people not much older than us marching, shouting, holding signs. "The Dotbusters inspired people to march and organize, to change anti–hate crimes laws."

"They even inspired the first Sikh mayor of Hoboken, Ravi Bhalla, to run for office!" I say, pointing to Mayor Bhalla's face on the screen. He's smiling through his beard beneath a neat blue turban that matches his suit. "I mean, he mentioned the Dotbusters in his acceptance speech when he became mayor."

Veda looks at Mayor Bhalla, and then, thoughtfully, at me. "He used all that hate against us and changed it into something good."

I think about what Veda just said about Mayor Bhalla. And of all the people who experienced much worse than me but didn't give up. They found a way not only to rage, but to fight back and rebuild something different and better. There were all these young people marching in the video. Even if they were scared, they weren't alone—they were out there, arm in arm, together.

"What is it Gandalf says to Frodo again?" I turn to Veda, feeling all that angry energy in my belly turning into something different.

Without missing a beat, my bestie smiles and says, "We can't change the times we live in, we can only decide what to do with the time that's given to us."

"Yeah!" I say, pumping my fist in the air. "That!"

And so, that's how it happens. I'm not saying it's because of *Lord of the Rings*, but definitely some mix of Gandalf, and Mayor Bhalla, my mom's activist friends, those desi kids who took to the streets, and even the racist yellers on the highway and my clueless substitute teacher. Because of all those forces, I decide to take my anger and turn it into something better. Something that won't make any of us feel alone but will celebrate how strong we all are together.

When we mention our plan to Ms. C., she gives us a secret smile and shows us a link to a viral video of some Asian American girls in California who formed a punk rock band and made art out of their own rage.

"Don't you girls have a band of your own?" the librarian asks. "You practice at the community center, right?"

Veda nods, smiling, but I watch the video with big eyes and an even bigger feeling of doubt growing in my stomach. "But we're nowhere as good as these girls!" I say. "I take that back, actually, Veda's amazing. But I couldn't pull off something like that!"

"Couldn't you?" Ms. C. asks with a mysterious smile before she wanders away again.

The march and fundraising fair are actually easy to organize, because the community center gives us a way to reach all our various communities. We talk to the dance and language classes, my dad's cricket team, my mom's women's group, the spelling bee folks, the singing and cooking classes, a mystery lovers' book club, and more. Those people we can't talk to, we print up flyers for—with Ms. Chandrashekhar's help, of course. Because, unfortunately, we still have that limit on how many copies we can each make at school. And our principal isn't interested in bending the rules for us, despite the worthwhileness of our cause.

"I guess bureaucracy stops for no woman," Veda grumbles.

"That sounds like a punk rock song," I tell her.

I'm joking, but she pulls out one of those really long drug store receipts from her pocket and writes down the phrase.

The day of the march is amazing. Bright and sunny without a cloud in the sky. There are hundreds of people starting at the school walking together all the way down to the community center with signs that say things like SAVE OUR COMMUNITY CENTER, MAPLE GROVE IS FOR EVERYONE, and THIS IS OUR HOME TOO.

Unlike that other morning at school, I'm not alone. My heart fills at the sight of all the grandparents and moms and dads and kids of all different colors walking hand in hand through our town. Ma warned us that maybe there'd be some haters, but the crowd is so beautiful and big and energetic, I certainly don't see or hear them if they are there. All I can hear and see are voices raised in solidarity and protest, faces full of energy, and fists reaching toward the sky. As we reach closer to the community center, the Panjabi bhangra troupe who promised to come for the fundraiser join the march, banging on their dhols in a wild rhythm. Then a bunch of Gujarati garba dancers come out of nowhere and begin doing a twirling stick-dance.

Ma had given me her rally bullhorn, and when I shout, “Stop asking us where we’re from!” our entire community shouts back, “We belong here!”

And when I yell, “Don’t tell us to go back where we’re from!” the crowd shouts back, “We belong here!”

I lean over to my bestie, whispering, “I don’t care anymore if racists are bad at geography.”

“Because who cares what they think anyway?” Veda asks, her face super red and sweaty from all the excitement.

“Yeah, but also because who needs them? Look at us! We have a whole community who has our back.” I gesture out to the crowd, spotting Ms. Chandrashekhar in a full-on white gi doing a tae kwon do exhibition with others from her class in front of the community center.

“We’re here!” Veda says, gesturing to the

community center gates, which are flung wide open, welcoming any and all inside.

A little bit later, I jump up on a makeshift stage with my best friend and the rest of our all-girl, newly punk rock band. It's the first time I haven't felt like I'm just keeping Veda company or faking my musical talent. I'm realizing I have a voice, and it grows stronger the more I use it for things I believe in. At first, my singing is soft and a little trembly, but it grows stronger with every word.

"Thank you for coming, everyone, to the Save Maple Grove Community Center rally and fund-raiser. As you can see, we are a strong community, made even more so by a center that welcomes us all." I have to stop then, because the cheers are so loud. "But the communities that use the center aren't just about food, or festivals, or dance, or spelling. We're also about building a better home here in Maple Grove for everyone!"

There are more cheers, and then we strike up the song we've been practicing all week. It's a punk rock anthem written by Veda and put to music by none other than yours truly.

"If you want to know where every brown person's *really* from," I sing as Veda and the other band members back me up. "If you regularly tell people to go back to where they came from..." I sing on.

"Hey, guess what? You're a bigot!" we all sing together in chorus.

"If you get a chai latte every morning before work but think the smell of real desi food is just the worst," I sing. "Hey, guess what? You're a bigot!"

"We're grandmas and tatas and babas and mas!" I go on, leaning into the mic, feeling the energy of the crowd expanding my heart, changing my anger into something even more powerful than love. "We're betis and bhaiyas and sisters and more!"

"We're not going anywhere! This is our community!" Veda sings into her microphone.

"You can't scare us, bigots! Together we are free!" I reply, grinning at her.

And then all together, we rock it out. There's bhangra and Odissi and tai chi and spelling bee champions and auntie feminists and cricketers and family and community. And we are all here, and we all belong.

Every day, with every breath, every song, every word, we redraw the map of a place called home. A home where we'll all always belong.

ACKNOWLEDGMENTS

There's something truly special about growing up as a South Asian American. Even though as a group we come from different countries, speak a multitude of languages, practice different religions, and have various ethnicities, we all have something in common: samosas! Well, samosas *plus* the fact that we are all proud to be desi, people originating from the Indian subcontinent, bonded by a shared history and culture.

I'll admit that I wasn't always as proud of my heritage when I was growing up as a Pakistani American child of immigrants in the 1970s and '80s. I didn't feel like I was fully American or that I belonged—no matter how badly I wanted that. But I clearly wasn't fully Pakistani, either. I faltered when I spoke Urdu or Panjabi, giggled at the wrong times during the Bollywood movies we rented, and felt self-conscious sharing my Pakistani side with friends at school.

I'm certain it didn't help that I never saw myself represented or included in the books I devoured as a kid. To make matters worse, in American TV shows and movies, the only references to my culture were jokes and stereotypes. Today, I can only imagine how much of a difference it might have made in my life if I had met Maha, Sanjay, Rahma, Veda, or the rest of the kids on the pages of this book. I'm sure I would have felt more confident and secure in my identity.

I do know that, as an adult, I felt a shiver when I first read *Rickshaw Girl* by Mitali Perkins and that I was hugely inspired by this groundbreaking desi author. I was moved by the beauty of *Shooting Kabul* by N. H. Senzai and amazed by how I could relate to the family being portrayed. I laughed out loud when reading a hilarious scene that Sayantani DasGupta wrote about dressing up as an Indian princess for Halloween in *The Serpent's Secret*. That was literally *me*, and my life, on the page! When I read the beautiful *The Night Diary* by Veera Hiranandani, I was flooded with emotion and thought of stories my father had shared from that terrible and critical time in our history.

I dreamed about creating an anthology that could bring our writing together, short stories linked into one greater story, but decided I would do it only if those writers, and others I admire greatly, would agree to be a part of it. I was hoping Rajani LaRocca, with her stunning verse in *Red, White, and Whole* and other marvelous works, would find the time to join us. I had fallen in love with Maulik Pancholy's debut novel, *The Best at It*, and knew his relatable, warmhearted, and funny characters needed to be included. Reem Faruqi, with her gentle, sweet narration, and the sensitivity of *Unsettled*, would be a wonderful addition. Supriya Kelkar had blown me away when we first met and she handed me a copy of *Ahimsa*, and I remain a huge fan of every book she's published since. I couldn't imagine a collection without Aisha Saeed, whose fantastic range of writing makes you feel every emotion possible, like in the unforgettable *Amal Unbound*. Finally, I took a leap and asked the brilliant Simran Jeet Singh, whose debut picture book, *Fauja Singh Keeps Going*, is such a winner, to try his hand at writing middle-grade fiction with me.

I can't properly express how grateful I am that every one of these amazing authors and humans trusted me with this project and agreed to join me on this journey. It was an incredible honor and joy to work with each one of them, to witness their creativity and passion for writing, and to help them craft and weave together these incredible stories into one interconnected piece that represents us all. We created the fictional Maple Grove, a place for our characters to live together, and the community center where the action unfolds, based on the personal connections we've all had in one way or another with real-life places like it.

I'm excited that kids today will grow up with books by these terrific authors—and many others that we unfortunately couldn't fit into one collection without making it at least six hundred pages long! I have no doubt their lives will be richer and happier for it.

This anthology would also not be possible without the wholehearted encouragement and support of Ellen Oh, who is a tireless advocate for inclusion and representation, and a wonderful mentor and friend.

Also, a big thank-you to agent Matthew Elblonk, acquiring editor Farrin Jacobs, our dedicated and supportive editor Erika Turner, and the exceptional team at Little, Brown Books for Young Readers for believing in this anthology and bringing it to life.

Finally, to all the readers out there, you are a part of our family. No matter what differences we have, and whatever happens across the world, American desis everywhere open our doors and hearts for each other and for anyone else who wants to join us. We will welcome you with samosas, chai, sweets, and maybe even flower garlands, because hospitality is one of our most cherished customs. And we are so happy to have you here with us, to share in our traditions, celebrations, rituals, rallies, and more. Because we are a community, all of us, together. And when we are with each other, we are home.

—Hena Khan

ABOUT THE CONTRIBUTORS

Veera Hiranandani is the Newbery Honor author of several books for young people. Her most recent middle-grade novel, *How to Find What You're Not Looking For*, received the Sydney Taylor Book Award and the Jane Addams Book Award and was a finalist for the National Jewish Book Award. She's also the author of the Phoebe G. Green chapter book series. A former book editor at Simon & Schuster, she's now a faculty member at Vermont College of Fine Arts. She lives in a little town on the Hudson River with her husband, two kids, and a very silly cat named Molly.

Maulik Pancholy is an award-winning actor, author, and activist. His acting career has spanned hit television shows (*30 Rock*, *Only Murders in the Building*), animated favorites (*Phineas and Ferb*, *Sanjay and Craig*), and the Broadway stage and films. His debut novel, *The Best at It*, was named a Stonewall Honor Book, and his second novel, *Nikhil Out Loud*, is a Lambda Literary Award winner. He served on President Barack Obama's Advisory Commission on Asian Americans and Pacific Islanders, and he is a cofounder of the anti-bullying nonprofit Act to Change. As a kid, Maulik danced his heart out at Navratri celebrations at his local community center. He now lives in Brooklyn, New York, with his husband, Ryan, and their adorable puppy, Arlo.

Aisha Saeed is a proud Punjabi Pakistani American *New York Times* bestselling author of books for young people. Some of her books include the middle-grade novel *Amal Unbound* and the picture book *Bilal Cooks Daal*, which received an Asian/Pacific American Award for Literature Honor. Aisha is also a founding member of the nonprofit We Need Diverse Books.

Mitali Perkins has written many books for young readers, including *You Bring the Distant Near* (nominated for a National Book Award) and *Rickshaw Girl* (adapted into a film), many of which feature children crossing different kinds of borders or explore justice themes like poverty, immigration, child soldiers, microcredit, affordable housing, and human trafficking. She lives and writes in the San Francisco Bay Area.

Reem Faruqi is the award-winning author of *Lailah's Lunchbox*, a picture book based on her own experiences as a young Pakistani American Muslim girl immigrating to the United States from the United Arab Emirates. She is also the author of the middle-grade books *Unsettled*, *Golden Girl*, and *Anisa's International Day*, and the picture books *Amira's Picture Day*, *I Can Help*, and *Milloo's Mind*. Like her character Amena in the story "Sweet and Sour," Reem loves watermelon-flavored Sour Patch gummies. Reem's latest book is *Call Me Adnan*.

Simran Jeet Singh is an award-winning activist, writer, teacher, and scholar who was recognized among *Time* magazine's 16 People Fighting for a More Equal America. He is the executive director for the Aspen Institute's Religion & Society Program and author of the national bestselling book *The Light We Give: How Sikh Wisdom Can Transform Your Life*. Simran's debut children's book, *Fauja Singh Keeps Going*, was named a National Public Radio Best Book and a New York Public Library Best Book and received a Christopher Award. Simran holds graduate degrees from Harvard University and Columbia University, and he is a regular contributor to multiple outlets, including *Time*, the *Washington Post*, and CNN.

Supriya Kelkar is a screenwriter and award-winning author and illustrator who grew up in Michigan, where she learned Hindi as a child by watching three Bollywood movies a week. Winner of the New Visions Award for her novel *Ahimsa*, Supriya has worked on the writing teams for several Hindi films. Supriya's books include *American as Paneer Pie*, about a Marathi American Hindu girl, loosely based in part on moments from her own childhood; *Strong as Fire, Fierce as Flame*; *Bindu's Bindis*; *That Thing about Bollywood*; *Brown Is Beautiful*; *The Cobra's Song*; *My Name*; and *And Yet You Shine: The Kohinoor Diamond, Colonization, and Resistance.*

Rajani LaRocca was born in India and raised in Kentucky, and now lives in the Boston area, where she practices medicine and writes award-winning books for young readers, including *Red, White, and Whole*, which received a Newbery Honor, the Walter Dean Myers Award, the New England Book Award, and more. A voracious reader, she never saw herself in a book until she was an adult, and now she writes stories about Indian American characters having adventures, contending with challenges, and experiencing joy. She writes fiction and nonfiction, novels and picture books, in prose and poetry. Rajani was once the features editor, and eventually the editor in chief, of her school newspaper.

N. H. Senzai is the author of *Shooting Kabul*, winner of the Asian/Pacific American Award for Literature and an NPR's

Backseat Book Club pick; as well as Edgar Award nominee *Saving Kabul Corner*; YALSA pick *Ticket to India*; *Escape From Aleppo*, recipient of the Middle East Book Award Honor; and *Flying Over Water.* She is currently working on two picture books, *Prince Among Slaves* and *Ice Cream Cornucopia.* She spent her childhood in San Francisco and Jubail, Saudi Arabia, and attended high school in London, where she was voted "most likely to read a literary revolution" due to reading comic books in class.

Hena Khan has been publishing books for children, including many that center Pakistani American characters like her, for over two decades. She is the author of the bestselling middle-grade novel *Amina's Voice*; *Amina's Song*, which won the Asian/Pacific American Award for Children's Literature; *Drawing Deena*; and *More to the Story*; and the Zayd Saleem, Chasing the Dream; Zara's Rules; and Super You! series, in addition to several acclaimed picture books. Born and raised in Maryland, Hena still lives near her old neighborhood and enjoys attending events at the local community center with her family.

Sayantani DasGupta is the *New York Times* bestselling author of the critically acclaimed Bengali folktale and string theory–inspired Kiranmala and the Kingdom Beyond books, the first of which—*The Serpent's Secret*—was a Bank Street Best Book of the Year, a *Booklist* Best Middle Grade Novel of the 21st Century, and an E. B. White Read Aloud Honor Book. She is also the author of the Fire Queen and Secrets of the Sky series and *She Persisted: Virginia Apgar*, as well as the young-adult novels *Debating Darcy* and *Rosewood: A Midsummer Meet Cute*. Sayantani is a pediatrician by training but now teaches at Columbia University and is a team member of We Need Diverse Books.